Can Melanie handle an out-of-control horse?

Clucking, Melanie urged Jinx to canter, and she was relieved when the horse responded willingly. For a few seconds she felt the cool morning wind on her cheeks and reveled in the sensation of riding her beautiful, if willful, new colt.

But her reverie was cut short when Dani, riding Rascal, came along on the outside. Immediately Jinx shook his head threateningly at Rascal and pulled to the right, intent on crowding the other horse.

"Watch him!" Dani shouted, riding evasively while Melanie fought to keep Jinx from cutting over.

"Sorry!" Melanie called back. Her words flew back down her throat when Jinx broke stride and did a few crow hops.

"That horse of yours isn't a racehorse. He's road rage on hooves," Joe muttered when he drew up. He glared at Jinx out of the corner of his eye.

"We'll show you a racehorse," Melanie said, her blood surging as she joined Joe and Dani, who were forming a starting line. Though Melanie took care to keep Jinx straight, the minute he got in line next to Fast Gun he swung his hindquarters toward the other colt and poised himself to launch a kick. Acting quickly, Melanie closed her hands on the reins and dug her heel sharply into his side, causing him to move away just in time.

"Jeez, you hate everyone," Melanie muttered to the colt. "Sorry," she added, glancing at Joe. But Joe merely shook his head in disgust. Melanie couldn't blame him.

Collect all the books in the Thoroughbred series

Collect all the books in the Ashleigh series

*coming soon

THOROUGHBRED

UNBRIDLED FURY

CREATED BY

JOANNA CAMPBELL

WRITTEN BY

KARLE DICKERSON

HarperEntertainment

An Imprint of HarperCollinsPublishers

📖 **HarperEntertainment**

An Imprint of HarperCollins*Publishers*

10 East 53rd Street, New York, NY 10022-5299

This is a work of fiction. The characters, incidents, and dialogue are products of the author's imagination and are not to be construed as real. Any resemblance to actual events or persons, living or dead, is entirely coincidental.

▦ Produced by 17th Street Productions,
an Alloy Online, Inc., company

HarperCollins books are available at special quantity discounts for bulk purchases for sales promotions, premiums, or fund-raising. For information please call or write: Special Markets Department, HarperCollins Publishers Inc., 10 East 53rd Street, New York, NY 10022-5299. Telephone: (212) 207-7528. Fax: (212) 207-7222.

ISBN 0-06-056634-5

HarperCollins®, 📖®, and HarperEntertainment™ are trademarks of HarperCollins Publishers Inc.

Cover art © 2003 by 17th Street Productions, an Alloy Online, Inc., company

First printing: December 2003

Printed in the United States of America

Visit HarperEntertainment on the World Wide Web at
www.harpercollins.com

❖ 10 9 8 7 6 5 4 3 2 1

1

"*WATCH OUT!*"

Eighteen-year-old Melanie Graham's head snapped up at the panicked shout. She ducked instinctively as the coffee shop waitress slipped and tilted toward her, tray flying. Two juice glasses careened toward the petite teenager and shattered on the floor. Melanie jumped up in time to grab the waitress's arm. Luckily, her quick move kept the woman from falling in a heap on top of the broken glass.

"Whoa," Melanie gasped, steadying the older woman and looking at the slick mess on the coffee shop floor. For a split second she regretted her decision to eat at Clockers Coffee Shop instead of at the Belmont racetrack kitchen, as she usually did. What if she had gotten injured and had never been able to race again? After all the riding accidents she'd been in, she could just picture her riding career ruined because she'd been hurt in a freak coffee shop accident.

Oh, Graham, don't be melodramatic, she scolded herself. Turning to the waitress, she asked, "Are you okay?"

The waitress caught her breath and nodded. "I'm so sorry. I guess there was some water or something on the tile that made me slip. You didn't get hit by any glass, did you?"

Melanie shook her head.

"You sure got out of the way quickly. Some reflexes!" the waitress exclaimed.

Melanie pushed her short blond hair back and grinned. "Yeah, I guess I do have 'em."

A jockey had better have at least a few decent reflexes, she thought. She grabbed some napkins so that she could help the waitress start to clean up.

"Thanks, but I don't want you touching this glass," the waitress said, waving Melanie back into her seat. "I'll get some help and bring you some more juice. In the meantime I'll take your order. What'll you have?"

Bursting into laughter, Melanie exclaimed, "Well, I *was* going to order the Super Slam Special, but I've changed my mind! I'll have the Railbird Special instead."

The waitress smiled tiredly at Melanie's joke while she scribbled the order onto a pad.

"And my cousin Christina will have the same," added Melanie. "She'll be here any minute."

The waitress nodded, turning toward the kitchen and calling loudly for someone to sweep up the floor by booth number three.

Melanie turned back to her *Daily Racing Form*, her heart still pounding. It pounded even more as she savored the write-up on the Suburban Handicap, which she had ridden in the day before. Melanie had been piloting a bay colt named Rush Street for Tall Oaks Farm, and they had placed in a thrilling three-way photo finish. The article was full of exciting details about Stormrider, the winning horse. It went on to compliment Melanie's ride in a way that made her practically blush with embarrassment.

Jockey Melanie Graham once again demonstrated the fearless form that's definitely becoming her trademark. She didn't flinch when Stormrider veered toward her mount and Matter of Time thundered up threateningly on the other side. "Graham's definitely got ice in her veins. Nothing scares her," claimed Stormrider's jockey after the race. "Some of us call her Ice Princess."

Ice Princess. Melanie considered the words while she watched the busboy clean up the shattered glass.

Ha, if only they knew! she thought, wincing. *A better name for me might be Super Chicken.* For a split second she stared at the last piece of glass and thought about the sound that her filly's leg had made when it snapped during the Kentucky Derby. Just the thought of Perfect Image's horrifying accident filled her with fear.

Don't go there again, Melanie commanded herself. She tried to shake off the horrible memory.

Glancing out the window, Melanie thought about her black three-year-old. The filly was now rehabilitating at Townsend Acres in Kentucky. Melanie had been with her round the clock at first, but now she had to get out and race again. She'd flown back to Belmont a few days earlier to keep Christina company and to ride. And she had booked another flight to Kentucky for the next day so that she could look in on her beloved horse again.

I hope she's making more progress, Melanie mused. The last time she'd worked with the filly, she'd been able to take her out for a short walk in the soft bluegrass. Image had been on tranquilizers, so she didn't risk reinjuring her leg.

The waitress returned, placing a glass of juice in front of Melanie. She set another across the table for Christina.

Where is Christina, anyway?

4

Melanie scanned the coffee shop but didn't see any sign of her. Melanie usually stayed at her record producer father's house, but he and his wife, Susan, had left for a trip. Now she was sharing a room with Christina at a nearby motel. When Melanie had left the room earlier, Christina was still half asleep, but she'd mumbled that she'd meet Melanie for breakfast in just a few minutes.

She ought to be here by now, Melanie thought. Both girls were used to getting up before dawn to exercise-ride. Even when they had the rare opportunity to sleep in, as they'd had that day, they couldn't stay in bed much past eight. But Christina *had* been exhausted after the previous day's big race. Maybe she wouldn't be awake for hours.

Just as Melanie decided that Christina wasn't coming after all, she spotted her cousin heading toward her.

"Hey, Mel," said Christina Reese, sliding into the booth. She wore no makeup, and her hair was swept up in a loose ponytail. "Why did you let me sleep so late?"

Melanie snorted. "You think it's easy to get you up? You were out like a light!"

Christina grinned and stretched luxuriously. "Well, it felt good to be lazy for once." Then her eyes locked on the *Daily Racing Form.* "So, did the press give us some good ink?"

Melanie nodded and thrust the paper under her

cousin's nose. "Read for yourself," she said.

She watched Christina's hazel eyes dance as she read the article.

"Wow," Christina said when she finished. "I like what they wrote about Matt, but you definitely got the lion's share of the praise, Ice Princess."

"Don't you 'Ice Princess' me," Melanie said ruefully. "You know how scared I am sometimes."

Christina swirled her juice. "Gee, do you think it has something to do with all the racetrack spills you've had, all the times you've been bruised, concussed, and hospitalized?" she asked sarcastically.

Melanie shrugged. "Those were nothing," she said almost inaudibly. "Nothing ever scared me as much as hearing Image's leg snap in the Derby. There's nothing like the fear of losing a horse."

"Tell me about it," Christina said with a sigh. "I didn't think I ever wanted to race again after Callie. Still, I got Matt out there in spite of everything, and we did well, so I guess that's a step in the right direction."

Melanie smiled. She knew how hard it had been for Christina to ride in the Suburban the day before. Christina was wrestling with her own fears, brought on most recently by a bad accident on a horse named Callie in the Riva Ridge Breeders' Cup. Shortly after that, Callie had had to be put down. Christina had been devastated. Even though it hadn't been Chris-

6

tina's fault, Melanie was aware how much guilt her cousin carried with her. It had taken a lot of courage for Christina to mount Matter of Time for the Suburban. But she'd ridden like a champ. Matt had taken third place in the prestigious race.

"You know," Melanie said thoughtfully, "I used to think that being brave meant that you didn't feel fear. Now I'm beginning to see it's more about facing fear and doing what you need to do anyway."

"Maybe," Christina replied, folding the paper. "Well, that was yesterday's race, and it's over and onward, I guess. It's time to figure out what's ahead."

"That's easy. More races, including the Dwyer Stakes this afternoon," Melanie said decisively, taking a forkful of food. Christina was trying to decide between being a jockey and going to college with the goal of going to vet school. Melanie had made up her mind a long time ago that she wanted to be a jockey. And she had never second-guessed her decision. She thought about the upcoming races she hoped she'd be riding in at this meet and then afterward at Saratoga. "If everything goes the way I want it to, I'm going to be amazingly busy for the rest of the summer."

"Yep, that's for sure. And now the question is, what's next for Star?" Christina mused. Her fiery chestnut, Wonder's Star, was still resting up at Whitebrook Farm after winning the third leg of the Triple

Crown at Belmont. It was time to consider the next move in his winning career. "I'm still kicking around the idea of the Travers Stakes. Of course, some people think I should put him to stud, but it's too soon for that. He's got more races to win!"

Melanie continued to chew, but suddenly she felt incredibly low.

"What's wrong, cuz?" Christina looked puzzled.

Melanie bit her lip. "Nothing," she mumbled. She didn't sound convincing, even to herself.

"You're not having problems with Jazz or anything, are you?" Christina asked, referring to Jazz Taylor, Melanie's boyfriend, who owned Image. "His tour's going well, right?" Jazz was touring with his band, Pegasus. He and his entourage had just left for Europe for the month of July.

"Things are fine with Jazz," Melanie said quickly. "Did I tell you that he worked out a deal with Brad to pay off Image's rehabilitation fees? Jazz is giving him an interest in Image's foal when she's bred to Celtic Mist."

Christina sucked in her breath. "You didn't! Is Jazz crazy? You know it's never a good idea to go into a partnership with Brad Townsend," she replied. Brad owned Townsend Acres, a rival Thoroughbred breeding and training operation that was located near

Christina's parents' farm, Whitebrook. He had been causing trouble for Christina and her parents for years. "Have you forgotten how much he tried to meddle with Star before he sold his half interest to me?"

Melanie cut her off. "No, how could I?" she said. "But you have to admit, Brad's been awfully good to me. He saved Image's life by opening up his medical facility so that she could get the care she needed. I can't ever forget that."

"True," Christina said grudgingly. "But you've gotta watch that guy like a hawk. He's definitely gonna expect payback."

Melanie grinned. "Don't I know it! He sure likes the attention he gets from having a Derby winner at Townsend Acres. And he's definitely been trying to take advantage. But don't worry. Jazz played it smart and kept a controlling interest. I'll be able to train the foal and ride it when it comes time to race."

"Cool," Christina said approvingly. "So then why are you bummed? That's good news."

Melanie scowled. "I'm not bummed." But she looked into her cousin's face. She knew she wasn't fooling Christina a bit. "It's—it's just that you can still race Star," she blurted out, ashamed of how envious she felt. "I know I should just be grateful that Image is alive, but the idea of never being able to race her

9

again . . . I don't know. Riding other people's horses is fun and all, but it's not the same."

Shaking her head, she looked out the window at the ivy-covered buildings surrounding the famous track.

Christina was silent for a moment. "I know what you're saying. It means so much more when you're riding a horse you love like crazy."

Both girls were silent for a few seconds, each lost in her own thoughts.

Finally Christina said, "Image will make one fabulous broodmare. Her lines are impeccable, and Celtic Mist's pedigree isn't anything to sneeze at. One day you're going to saddle up her foal. If I know you, you'll never look back."

"I'm definitely looking forward to racing Image's baby. The trouble is, it's not going to be for years, even if everything goes perfectly," Melanie reminded her. "What am I going to do in the meantime?"

"You're going to be patient, jockey a zillion other horses, and make a name for yourself. That way you'll be ready to take on a fresh challenge," Christina said. "You'll need it, too. With Image as its dam, that foal will probably have a pretty fiery temperament!"

Melanie smiled weakly at her cousin's attempt to buoy her spirits. "You know me—patience isn't exactly my strength."

"Hmmm," Christina said, drumming her fingers

10

on the table. "I guess you're right. You need a project to throw your heart into right away. So it's simple. We just have to find you a new horse—and soon."

"Yeah," Melanie said. "But it can't be just *any* horse, you know."

"I know." Christina nodded.

"It has to be special," Melanie added. *Special like Image*, she thought with a gulp, thinking of her high-spirited black filly. Image could be stubborn and a handful at times, but when she was on the track, she ran like the wind. She was that rare combination of Thoroughbred brilliance, fire, and speed.

From the time Melanie had first set eyes on the beautiful filly, she had known that Image was different from other horses she had ridden. Never mind that she could be willful and unpredictable. Never mind that even loading her into a trailer could be a real challenge at times. Even though Image had tested Melanie's patience and skills to the limit, Melanie had known that she was a true winner in every way. Her victory in the Kentucky Derby had only underscored Melanie's deep belief in her.

"She sure ran well in the Derby, didn't she?" Melanie smiled wistfully. She had spent a great deal of time reliving the horrible moment when Image's leg had gotten broken. She really hadn't thought much about her glorious run beforehand.

Christina nodded. "She was amazing."

Just then the waitress thrust the bill under Melanie's nose. Melanie sighed as she stood up. "Since we took off the whole morning, I suppose we'd better get a move on and go see to the horses," she said.

After the girls left the coffee shop, they walked quietly toward Belmont's backside. It was a hot July day. The New York air was heavy with humidity. Now that it was almost lunchtime, the workouts were finished. Men driving tractors harrowed the track, preparing for the afternoon races. The stable area was quiet for a brief period. It would be at least an hour before trainers and grooms started readying the horses to run.

"It was weird not exercise-riding this morning," Melanie said aloud as they walked along the shed rows.

"Yeah," agreed Christina. "Though I'm not sure I could have even thrown my leg over a saddle. I don't know about you, but every muscle group in my body aches."

Melanie nodded. "Yeah, I'm pretty tired myself, and my legs feel like rubber. I just hope I can stay aboard Maplewood this afternoon in the Dwyer. I can see the headlines now: 'Ice Princess Melts Before Record Crowd at Belmont.'"

Christina laughed lightly while Melanie paused to pat a friendly bay gelding who had thrust his muzzle toward her. His stall door was open, his stall guard stretched across the opening. Melanie studied the gelding's gleaming coat for a moment. She noted how fit and well cared for he seemed to be.

"Someone probably loves you a lot, huh, sweet boy?" she murmured, giving the horse a last scratch under his jaw before walking on.

Just the way I love Image, she thought. She turned toward the row of stalls that housed the Whitebrook horses.

As she drew closer to the stalls Melanie felt her heart grow heavier and heavier. It was amazing how different things looked that day. Less than twenty-four hours before, she'd been on top of the world, thrilled that she'd ridden so well in the Suburban. She'd been dreaming of racing successes to come. Now she couldn't face the thought of climbing aboard horses that belonged to other people.

Without a horse of your own, racing is fun, but it's just not the same, she repeated to herself bleakly.

Suddenly Melanie stopped, overcome by a horrible thought. Christina turned toward her, concern written across her face.

"You still worried about what's next?" Christina asked gently.

Melanie nodded. Then she blurted out, "Oh, Chris, what if I *never* find another horse like Image? It could

13

happen, you know. I could just go on and on riding horses forever, but never having that . . . that *connection* ever again!"

"You'll never replace Image," Christina said, reaching over to hug Melanie. "But I know you'll find another special horse that you'll connect with. I just know it."

"I hope you're right," Melanie replied slowly.

2

IT WAS QUIET AT BARN NINE. MELANIE LOOKED IN ON THE Whitebrook horses that were stabled there for the meet. March to Glory, Ending Shadows, and Charisma all dozed in their stalls. The barn area was clean and freshly raked. A couple of grooms sat around cleaning tack. Since Whitebrook had no horses running in the afternoon races, they didn't have that much work to do. Even Ian McLean, Whitebrook's head trainer, dozed in a lawn chair with several racing schedules in his lap.

Christina gestured toward a heap of freshly laundered bandages. "Good, someone's just washed all the bandages," she said, evidently glad to find something to do.

Melanie looked around, wishing that she could be useful, too.

"Guess I'll go over to Dreamflight and look in on Maplewood," she told her cousin. "And I probably ought to see if I can go scare up some more rides before I zip home to Kentucky to see Image. My dance card is kind of open for the rest of this meet, and I don't have much lined up for Saratoga yet, either."

"I wouldn't worry about it. You're a Derby winner, a hot commodity. You'll be turning down offers," Christina said.

That thought lifted Melanie's spirits a little. All she'd ever wanted was to become a jockey. Now that high school was behind her, she was free to pursue her dream full-time.

Melanie turned toward barn four, where Dreamflight's horses were stabled. She had just stopped in front of Maplewood's stall when she saw Amanda Johnston approach her.

"There you are, Melanie. I was just coming over to try to find you," said Amanda, who along with her husband, Patrick, owned the training facility. "Bad news. Patrick is over scratching Maplewood for the Dwyer."

"Why?" Melanie was stunned. The last time she'd ridden him, he'd been fit and bursting with health.

Amanda bit her lip and shook her head. She toyed

absently with a lock of her blond hair. "He turned up lame this morning. We're not sure what's wrong. The track vet took some X rays. I imagine we'll find out pretty quickly."

Melanie could tell that Amanda was upset. She and her husband had come all the way to New York from California with several promising horses. Melanie knew that she was hoping to make a name for Dreamflight at Belmont. Matt's third-place show in the Suburban had been notable, but another win in the grade 2 stakes on Maplewood would have been nice for the farm. Plus, Melanie knew, the $150,000 purse wouldn't have been bad, either.

When Amanda left after patting Maplewood on the nose, barn four seemed deserted. Only Jessica, the groom, was around. She wrapped Noble Answer's legs while she whistled tunelessly. It was clear to Melanie that the groom wasn't in any mood to talk. She nodded briefly at Melanie but didn't stop slowly winding the thick wraps around Nobie's left hind leg, making sure to apply pressure evenly. Melanie could see that she was being careful not to leave any bumps. Idly Melanie watched Jessica for a few moments, then let out a sigh and wandered down the shed row.

Scowling as she walked, Melanie felt her mood plummeting even more. Though she was tired, she'd been looking forward to running in the Dwyer that afternoon. Now she could only ride the Suburban over and over in her mind.

That was the trouble with a big race, Melanie decided. After all the excitement, she usually felt a letdown. But this time it was worse than usual, she decided. Maybe it was because now that Image was no longer racing, she just didn't seem to have anything specific to look forward to. No doubt about it—Melanie was incredibly bored, and being bored was something she absolutely couldn't stand.

Well, I'll just have to fix that, she decided, walking on.

For the rest of the afternoon she made it a point to look in on various trainers and chat for a while. She made every effort to remind them that she was always available to ride. She really didn't like having to sell herself or bring up some of her recent wins. But it was all part of the game. One or two trainers took her card, but several acted as though they had winning jockeys to spare. They didn't seem to take her seriously.

"Your boss doesn't think much of me, considering my racing record," Melanie grumbled to one of the trainer's stable hands after the trainer turned her down outright and disappeared to take a phone call.

"Could be he thinks that your winning the Derby was simply a matter of luck," said the stable hand, sneering a little.

"Was my second in the Belmont Stakes just luck as well?" Melanie asked. She hated to brag, but she also hated to be written off for no reason.

"You haven't been riding that long. The Belmont could have been just more beginner's luck," the stable hand replied.

"Maybe," Melanie said with a grin, looking pointedly at a horseshoe that someone had nailed over the feed room door. "But in this business horseshoes aren't enough. It also helps to have people ride for you who happen to be lucky."

Still, by the end of the day Melanie decided that maybe luck was on her side after all. She'd gotten a well-respected trainer named Andy Chalon to agree to let her ride his horse in the Bowling Green Handicap the following week. The Bowling Green Handicap was another grade 2 race. It was open to three-year-olds and up. Andy's horse, Bayleaf, was older, but one look at him showed Melanie that the horse still had plenty of races left in him.

"Great, I'm looking forward to riding Bayleaf," Melanie said to the gray-haired man. She shook his gnarled hand. "I have to fly home to Kentucky for a few days and see my horse. Then I'll be back here on Saturday to ride for you," she told the trainer.

After saying good-bye, Melanie walked back to the motel. She opened the door to let herself into her room.

"I'm in the tub," called Christina from behind the closed door of the bathroom.

"I figured that's why it's doubly humid in here," Melanie replied, flopping onto the sofa. Picking up the TV remote, she flipped through the channels but didn't really watch.

I'm so bored, I could scream, she thought. She pressed the OFF button and stared at the blank screen.

Just then the phone rang, and Melanie pounced on it. She hoped it wasn't a reporter who wanted another follow-up story about the Suburban. Though the race had happened only the day before, she was already over it. She was ready to move on. Too bad she didn't know where exactly she was going to move on to.

"Hello?" she said warily. She smiled when she heard the scratchy connection and the sound of Jazz's voice. "Where are you?"

"I'm in France," he exclaimed, his voice bright.

Melanie felt her heart lift. Jazz's voice was the best thing she'd heard all day. She pictured him in her mind, his dark good looks and his longish hair in a ponytail.

"How's the tour going?" she asked, curling up in the corner of the sofa. She couldn't wait to hear everything.

"Really well. We had an outrageous night. The place was packed. Ticket sales hadn't been going so well. But suddenly, at the last minute, we were swamped. We almost sold out. I wish you could have been there. We rocked!"

Melanie smiled. "I wish I'd been there, too," she responded, toying with the cord.

"If things keep going this way, Pegasus will be in great shape financially," Jazz said.

"That's cool," Melanie replied. She was glad for Jazz. She knew he'd been troubled about finances. Then he'd had to figure out how to pay Image's rehabilitation fees. Now if his ticket sales started to take off, things would be much easier for Jazz in the money department.

"So tell me, how did the Suburban go?" Jazz asked.

Melanie filled him in on the details. She was pleased to hear how happy Jazz sounded that she'd ridden well. It sure was nice that Jazz could be so supportive, considering how busy and stressful his own schedule was. But after she told him about the big race, her voice trailed off. There just didn't seem to be anything more to say.

"So things went well, but you sound a little down, Graham," Jazz said.

"Not really," Melanie replied, chewing on her lip. "Well, a little, I guess. I'm just wondering what's next. Now that the big races are over, there doesn't seem to be much to look forward to."

21

"Are you kidding? What about this fall?" Jazz exclaimed.

"Fall?" Melanie was puzzled.

"You know, when we go horse shopping. You haven't forgotten about that, have you?"

"Of course not," Melanie said with a snort.

"We'll hit all the big auctions," Jazz continued. "We'll have a blast looking for the next big thing, don't you think?"

Melanie nodded as she said, "I *am* looking forward to finding another horse. There's just one problem. What if we don't find one like Image?"

Jazz laughed. "Of course we won't find another Image, but don't worry. We'll find a great horse. I just know it."

"Yeah," Melanie said, remembering that her cousin had said practically the same thing. Still, she wasn't convinced. "It's just that Image is a pretty tough act to follow. She was everything wrapped up in one neat package. Fire and spirit and a will to win and—and everything." Her voice got choked up and she couldn't go on. It still didn't seem possible to take in the fact that Image would never race again.

"You listen to me, Graham," Jazz said, sounding serious. "Image is one fabulous horse, and we still have her. Don't lose sight of that. But there are other incredible horses out there, and we're going to find one that'll make the racing world take notice. Don't doubt it for a second."

"Yeah, I guess you're right," Melanie said more strongly. She wanted to believe it. She *had* to believe it. If she didn't, there was nothing left.

"There's just one thing," Jazz added.

"What's that?" Melanie sat up straight, wondering what was coming.

"Uh, next time, let's get a horse that's a little calmer," Jazz said. "Fire and brilliance are one thing, but you have to admit that Image had more than her fair share of the fireworks part of it."

Melanie chuckled, thinking of all of Image's antics over the last few months. Sometimes she'd wondered if she'd taken on more than she could handle. "Yeah, you're right about that," she agreed.

"So when we choose our next horse," Jazz went on, "we're going to look for one that's fast but less complicated than Image."

"Fair enough," Melanie agreed before hanging up.

3

"OH, IF IT ISN'T MY LITTLE OLD KENTUCKY HOME," MELANIE said wryly under her breath. She glanced at the luxurious grounds of Townsend Acres as she pulled up to the guard gate and announced herself.

It was Monday, and Melanie had left Belmont that morning after workouts to fly to Kentucky. She'd hoped to make it back to the farm in time to be able to work Image that afternoon, but there had been a security alert at the airport. The resulting two-hour delay had nearly driven Melanie crazy, because it meant she wouldn't arrive at Townsend Acres in time to take Image out for her daily walk. It was now dusk, and the clouds were glowing bright pink in the evening sky.

Melanie tapped her fingers impatiently against the

steering wheel as the guard punched her name into the computer.

It's not like he doesn't know who I am, Melanie thought irritably. She stuck her tongue out at the video camera mounted overhead as she waited for her clearance to pop up on the screen. Sometimes she wanted to scream at the way things were run at Townsend Acres. Everything was high-security these days. While it was understandable considering how valuable Brad Townsend's horses were, sometimes it was a real pain.

But soon she was on her way, driving through Townsend Acres' beautifully landscaped grounds. She drove past several expansive barns and parked the Blazer she shared with Christina in front of a yellow guest cottage. Brad had graciously let her use the cottage while Image was recovering at the farm's state-of-the-art medical facility.

Letting herself in with her key, Melanie dumped her duffel bag by the front door. She put on her paddock boots, grabbed a carrot, and headed for Image's stall, which was in a stable attached to the rehabilitation barn. Her steps quickened as she drew closer.

"Image, I'm back," she called.

From the closed stall, Melanie could hear Image's shrill nicker. Melanie hated that the stall had to be closed to other horses and visitors, but she knew that it was necessary for health and security reasons. Still,

25

now that Image was making such progress in her recovery, she was itching to move the filly. She wanted to put her in a stall where she wouldn't be cut off from everything. Image didn't like to be confined.

I need to really start thinking about having Image taken over to Whitebrook, Melanie thought. She undid the latch and slowly opened the heavy wooden stall door. Townsend Acres was definitely a top-notch facility, but Melanie knew that her beloved filly belonged at Whitebrook. *The heck with what Dr. Seymour says. I don't see why I have to wait till the end of the month.*

"Easy, girl," Melanie said when she caught her first glimpse of Image, who was crowding the door, nickering. The gorgeous black filly's well-shaped ears were pricked, and her nostrils were flared. She was glad to see Melanie.

"Oh, girl, I missed you," Melanie exclaimed, throwing her arms around her horse's shiny neck. She buried her face in Image's silky mane and breathed in the scent of hay and horse. There was nothing like it in the whole world, she decided.

Standing back, Melanie smiled as she gazed into Image's soft brown eyes. She saw how good the filly looked. She'd maintained her needed weight, and her alert expression showed that she was in high spirits. Her groom, Marcos, had obviously taken good care of her.

Melanie was relieved. She had hated to trust Image's care to anyone else, even a sweet guy such as Marcos. But after Christina's disastrous ride on Callie, Melanie had had no choice but to return to Belmont to bolster her cousin. What's more, Melanie had known she had to stay for a while and maintain a visible presence. This was necessary if she was going to go after her dream of being a jockey.

"But the next few days are reserved just for you, girl," Melanie told Image happily. Now that she was back with her horse, nothing else seemed to be very important.

Suddenly Image threw up her head and pawed at her thick bedding.

"No pawing. What is it, girl?" Melanie asked. Just then she heard the sound of approaching footsteps.

"I saw your Blazer pull up at the gate, and I thought I'd find you here."

Looking up, Melanie saw that it was Brad Townsend. He stepped across the stall opening. The dim lights of the barn played across his chiseled, aristocratic features. He was dressed in a black tuxedo, which struck Melanie as ridiculous against the backdrop of the barn. Still, that was how Brad always looked: overdressed and above it all.

Melanie glanced at the tall, dark-haired man. "Hello," she said, making a conscious effort to look him in the eye. Lately it was hard to know how to react to Brad. He was always arrogant and dismissive of Melanie. But when he'd surprised everyone by allowing Image to come to his farm for rehabilitation, she hadn't known how to handle his unexpected gesture.

"Well, what do you think of Image?" Brad asked proudly.

Melanie grinned. "She looks fabulous," she replied.

"Well, of course she does. I've got a state-of-the-art facility and Dr. Dalton, the best veterinarian in Kentucky. She's got the best care in the state, maybe even the country," Brad bragged.

Inwardly Melanie smiled at his boasting. Outwardly, however, she didn't give any sign that she noticed. As long as Image was doing well, that was all that mattered. Let Brad brag all he wanted to about her miraculous recovery.

"She's scheduled for more water therapy tomorrow," Brad said. "But she's been hand-walked a fair amount, and she's coming along nicely."

Melanie knelt down in the straw and ran her hand lightly down Image's left leg. It was covered with a thick wrap to protect the still-tender area over the surgical implant. The implant had been needed to repair Image's break. "That's great," she said, frowning at the wrap. She thought about the filly's cannon bone, which would never be the same.

When Melanie stood up and dusted off her jeans, she could see that Brad was brushing a piece of hay off his jacket. His expensive gold watch gleamed in the soft barn light.

"I'd best be off," he said. "Lavinia and I are on our way to a little soiree at Paul Ashworth's place tonight."

"Soiree?" Melanie repeated, a lightbulb going off inside her head.

Brad gave her a disdainful look. "That's French for 'party.'"

What a show-off, she thought. *As if I didn't know what a soiree was!*

Brad went on. "Only Lexington's heavyweights have been invited. See you around."

Melanie suddenly pictured the engraved invitation she'd been sent three weeks earlier. She'd totally forgotten about it. She watched Brad swagger down the wide concrete aisle, and she laughed when he stepped in a pile of manure someone had forgotten to sweep up.

So much for those patent-leather shoes of his, she thought. *Serves the pompous jerk right. I'll bet it never occurred to him that maybe I was invited to the Ashworths' fancy party.*

29

Paul Ashworth was a local breeder, and he and his wife were prominent members of Lexington society. Normally people of their social position wouldn't even notice a teenager such as Melanie. But after she'd won the Kentucky Derby the Ashworths had made it a point to send her a congratulatory flower arrangement at the hospital. They'd also sent a get-well card. Shortly thereafter they'd sent Melanie the party invitation, which she'd been surprised to receive. But she'd been distracted by Image's injury and then Christina's accident, and the whole thing had slipped her mind.

Who cares? she thought, scratching Image's jaw.

Of course she wouldn't go. Melanie liked parties well enough, but not the kind where Lexington society gathered and didn't seem to do anything but posture for each other and flash their jewels. She ticked off more reasons not to go: She'd just flown back from an exhausting couple of weeks at Belmont. And she didn't have anyone to go with. What's more, she hadn't sent in a reply. Anyway, she just wanted to stay right there with Image.

But a few minutes later, when she saw how peacefully Image was dozing, she found herself thinking about the party. She pictured the owners, trainers, and other horse people who would be there—horse people who just might need someone like Melanie to climb aboard their horses and give them a whirl around a racetrack.

Letting herself out of Image's stall quietly, Melanie closed the door and fastened the latch.

The last thing she felt like doing was getting dressed up. But she knew she ought to put in an appearance, even if she hadn't sent in a response. It wasn't smart to snub the racing crowd. Anyway, if she wanted to get more rides, it wouldn't hurt to get her face out where it would be seen.

Twenty minutes later Melanie was back in the guest cottage desperately scrounging through her closet, looking for something she could wear to a formal party filled with adults. Finally, shoved in between several pairs of jeans, she found a pair of black silk pants. When she rooted around more, she found a cream-colored top she'd worn to a recent concert. Then she smiled when she saw a shimmery deep-green silky jacket she'd bought but never worn. It was perfect.

After quickly applying some lip gloss and a couple of strokes of mascara, Melanie combed back her hair and gelled it liberally. She shrugged as she gave herself a last glance in the mirror.

"This is as good as it gets," she murmured to her reflection.

Pausing by the phone, Melanie noticed that the

31

answering machine light was blinking, but she didn't want to take the time to retrieve her messages. She briefly considered calling a guy friend to go with her. But she couldn't think of anyone who'd be up for a last-minute formal party with a bunch of society types. It really wasn't fair to sentence anyone else to a yawn of an evening just so she could drum up some rides.

So what if I'm by myself? Plenty of people go solo. I'll only stay for a little while, Melanie told herself. She walked out into the summery night and headed for her car.

When Melanie pulled up in front of the Ashworths' stately mansion a half hour later, she saw that the Ashworths had hired a valet service for the evening. The elegantly uniformed staff was using lighted sticks to guide the luxurious cars headed up the drive toward the valet station.

"Uh-oh," Melanie mumbled to herself, glancing down in embarrassment at the interior of the Blazer she shared with Christina. It was filled with pieces of hay, magazines, and tack that she'd meant to take to the tack repair shop. She knew the outside of the car looked no better. It was covered with dust, and though it had been repaired since the accident she'd had recently, it now sported several new dings and dents.

Melanie quickly veered off the driveway and pulled around to the side by the stable area. She would park herself. There was no way she wanted anyone to see her wreck of a car.

Just as she climbed out of her Blazer, evening bag in hand, she saw a familiar truck pull up next to hers. Kevin McLean jumped out and called out to her.

"What are you doing here?" Melanie gasped in surprise.

Kevin's dad, Ian McLean, was head trainer at Whitebrook. Though Kevin used to exercise-ride for Whitebrook, these days he focused on soccer. The last place Melanie had expected to see him at was a gathering of racing people.

"Parking. My car smells like an old gym locker, and I'm not about to advertise the fact by letting anyone else drive this beast. What are you doing here?" Kevin asked. "I thought you were allergic to formal parties."

Melanie grinned. "I am. But I thought I'd better show my face and remind people that I'd love to be the one to take their horses across the finish line—preferably in first place."

Kevin gave her a squeeze around the shoulders. "You little opportunist," he teased Melanie. "My dad is in Belmont holding down the fort for Ashleigh and Mike, and he asked me to represent the family. So here I am."

Melanie glanced up at the huge southern-style home, now bathed in the glow of twinkling lights. The doors to the veranda were thrown wide open, and she could hear lively music drifting over toward the stables.

"Ugh, I hate these things," she muttered. She steeled herself to walk toward the grand house.

"Aw, they're not so bad. Where's your boyfriend?" Kevin asked.

"In Europe," Melanie replied. "Where's your girlfriend?"

Kevin grinned and held out his elbow. "Lindsay's off at some soccer tournament. Looks like we're each alone. I tried to call your place, but you didn't answer your phone, so I'll ask you now. Care to stand in as my date for the evening?"

"Sure, as long as you don't mind watching me kiss up to people so I can ride their horses," Melanie said, taking his arm. She and Kevin had dated a long time ago. Now they were friends who were as comfortable around each other as brother and sister.

She and Kevin walked up to the house and stepped into the vast entryway. They shook hands with the formally attired Ashworths, who were greeting their guests.

"So glad you could come," Mrs. Ashworth cooed, sweeping down to air-kiss Melanie. Melanie held her breath so that she wouldn't choke on the expensive perfume wafting around her.

"Did you see that blank look? Mrs. Ashworth

doesn't even know who I am," Melanie whispered a few seconds later to Kevin when they were out of earshot.

"That's okay," Kevin said with a light laugh. "Once she asks her people who you are, she'll be sure to come over to talk with you. Then she'll make a big deal about knowing the winner of the Kentucky Derby."

Melanie blushed. "You're probably right," she said with a sigh. It was good to get recognition for winning, but sometimes it was kind of weird to be the object of so much attention. Still, Melanie knew, her winning record was the thing that could help her to get more rides. It was all a matter of putting her face in front of people—on the track and at parties like these.

"Let the games begin," she murmured, tucking her hair behind her ears. She followed Kevin toward a glittering crystal punch bowl. Looking around, she tried to spot any horse owners who would have a mount she might be interested in. Instead, she caught a glimpse of Lavinia Townsend. Dripping with diamonds as usual, she was sipping from a champagne flute and laughing shrilly with some old guy who looked like a mobster. Quickly moving past Lavinia, Melanie saw a few familiar faces, but no one jumped out immediately as a possibility.

Hmmm, just the usual crowd, Melanie thought with disappointment. She eyed the actors, socialites, and other horse-racing figures she'd known for years. *Maybe it was a waste coming here after all.*

"It's not happening," Melanie said to Kevin after he'd said hello to some old family friends and turned back toward her.

"I wouldn't be so quick to jump to conclusions. Check it out," Kevin said, gesturing with his chin as he filled her punch cup. "Isn't that Harv Pressman? Didn't he just come out of nowhere to buy that big-deal colt that everyone's so hot on? What was his name?"

"Fail-safe," Melanie supplied automatically, reaching for the cup. "I read about it in the sports section a few weeks ago. He paid too much for the horse, but Fail-safe does have some promise. And I hear Harv Pressman's a nice guy."

"I'll bet he needs a jockey," Kevin said, playfully pushing her in the owner's direction.

Melanie grinned. "I'll bet he does. Wish me luck."

"Go, Melanie! Go, Melanie!" Kevin chanted in a singsong voice.

Glaring at Kevin, Melanie started walking toward the heavyset, balding man. He stood near a column topped with an imposing bronze sculpture of a Thoroughbred. As she drew closer she plastered on her brightest smile.

She had to rehearse for this intro: "Hi, Mr. Pressman. I'm Melanie Graham, and if you ever need a jockey for that fabulous new horse of yours, well, here's my card," she whispered to herself. She fumbled in her purse to find one of her cards so that she'd have it handy. She'd recently had cards printed up with her name and number for just such an occasion. Clutching a card, she moved in.

Okay, Mr. P., you're about to meet that winning jockey you've been waiting for, Melanie thought. Unfortunately, just as she was about to step in front of the man, a tall, beautiful, bejeweled woman approached him, immediately engaging him in conversation.

So much for that. Sighing, Melanie ducked behind a towering potted plant. *I'll just have to wait till he's finished,* she thought. She sipped from her punch cup and watched for a break in the conversation.

"So old Richard Maynard's washed up, eh? You say he's selling everything?"

Melanie froze as she heard Brad Townsend's voice from behind her. Turning her head slightly and peering through the leaves of the potted plant, she saw him. He held a crystal glass and leaned casually against a door frame while he talked with a tall man.

"Selling it all. I heard they started liquidating this morning. Unfortunately, I couldn't get out there," the man replied quietly. "I'm surprised you haven't heard. I figured you'd be the first one there, offering to buy Flag's Up Farm cheaply. At the very least, I thought, you'd want to snap up some of Maynard's prized bloodstock."

Brad laughed coldly. "Oh, believe me, if I needed any more horse farms or any more winning horses, I'd have known about it all before anyone else had heard the rumors. Thing is, I've got so many winners in my stables these days. I've got Celtic Mist and King's Ransom, to name two. I just don't have room for more."

Melanie looked down at her sandals. How could Brad brag that way all the time and not feel the tiniest bit of embarrassment? She freaked out whenever she had to mention one of her own accomplishments, even when it was necessary to her livelihood. Yet Brad could go on and on about himself even when it made no difference at all.

"I don't know, Townsend," the man replied, raising his drink in salute. "No matter how many winners you're saddled with, it never hurts to add another horse or two with great bloodlines to your collection—just for extra insurance."

"I don't need insurance," Brad said confidently.

"Well, some of us do," exclaimed the other man, clinking the ice cubes in his glass. "I hear Maynard had a horse or two with Seabiscuit bloodlines."

Seabiscuit! Melanie's ears perked up at the famous name. She had done a book report on him in middle school. Seabiscuit was a rough little bay that was one of America's premier racing legends. He had won all kinds of important races in the 1930s and '40s against all kinds of odds. When his racing days were over, he was retired to stud. However, few of his descendants had ever made much impact on the track, Melanie remembered from her reading—a fact that Brad was quick to point out to his friend.

"You'd do better buying a colt with Celtic Mist's bloodlines," Brad added.

After Brad started working on the man to breed one of his mares to his prized stallion, Melanie lost interest in the conversation. Then she suddenly remembered why she was at the party in the first place—to try to get rides, not to listen to idle talk about dispersal sales. When she glanced over toward Harv Pressman, she realized that the man had disappeared into the crowd.

"If you snooze, you lose, Graham," she scolded herself, walking back over to Kevin. He was talking with some other friends of his family. "Well, at least someone accomplished what he was supposed to this evening," she muttered under her breath. She wriggled her toes in her too-tight sandals and wished she could just go home. She'd rather work a horse than a party room any day.

• • •

"Talk about a great big waste of an evening," Melanie grumbled to Kevin as they left the party and started toward their cars.

"An evening with me—a waste? I'm hurt!" Kevin joked. Seeing Melanie's look, he ruffled her hair. "Aw, come on," he cajoled. "An evening of fine dining on weird gourmet food, old folks' music, a bunch of stuck-up rich people, and me for company? How can you call all that a waste of an evening?"

Melanie grinned. She had to admit it was fun to hang out with Kevin for old times' sake, even if she hadn't enjoyed any of the food or been able to catch any rides.

"Well, good night," she said, climbing into her Blazer. She waved as she drove off toward Townsend Acres.

While she drove, Melanie rolled down her windows and gazed at the starry sky. Soon she was lost in thought, picturing Image's foal. She imagined herself training the foal. When she suddenly came back to reality, she realized she'd passed the turnoff for Townsend Acres. She had no idea how far she'd driven.

Oh, great. Maybe I can add "got lost" to my list of things that went wrong tonight, Melanie thought sarcastically. She drove to the next exit and turned down an unfamiliar road. *I'll look for a driveway, turn around in it, and get back on the highway,* she thought. But suddenly a large FOR SALE sign at the side of the road caught her eye. The sign was erected on a stone wall with a brass plaque that read FLAG'S UP FARM. Next to the sign Melanie saw a large dispersal sale banner.

"That's the dispersal sale Brad and his friend were talking about," she said aloud, peering closer.

Melanie turned into the driveway and pulled back out. *Maybe I ought to stop by tomorrow and take a look. Just because Brad has too many winners in his stable doesn't mean I have to overlook a possibility.*

4

THE NEXT MORNING MELANIE WAS UP BEFORE FIRST LIGHT.
Throwing on her jeans and grabbing an apple for
breakfast, she made her way to the barn. She glanced
at the training oval off in the distance, bustling with
activity. Sighing, she turned toward the rehabilitation
barn. When she was outside Image's stall, Melanie saw
that Townsend Acres' vet, Dr. Dalton, had already
checked on the filly on his morning rounds. His
scratchy handwritten notes were clipped to the board
hanging on the wall.

"'Continued hydrotherapy. Light hand-walking,'"
Melanie read. *Nothing new here*, she thought. Sighing,
she noted the dosage of the tranquilizer that Dr. Dalton
had indicated to be administered before Image was

taken from her stall. Melanie hated giving Image tranquilizers, but she knew the filly had to be sedated or she might injure her leg again.

The filly thrust her nose into Melanie's palm the minute she threw back the stall door.

"Careful, greedy girl," Melanie exclaimed, laughing as the filly snatched the last bite of her apple. "You're on a strict diet, and we can't mess it up."

Carefully she took off Image's blanket, noting how edgy the filly was that morning.

Too many weeks of hardly exercising since her injury, Melanie thought, fighting back tears as she always did whenever she considered Image's condition. Pursing her lips, she poured the supplements containing Image's medication into her bin.

Later, when Melanie was sure that the tranquilizer had had time to work, she gently took off Image's blanket and hung it on the blanket rail in front of her stall. Then she carried her grooming box over to the thickly padded crossties. After returning to Image's stall and placing a green halter on the filly, Melanie led her slowly out of the stall and over to the crossties. Taking no chances, she guided the filly into the crossties but didn't attach the ties to her halter. Instead, she clipped the ties in front of Image and held her lead while she worked.

First Melanie brushed Image slowly and rhythmically, admiring the filly's powerful lines and stunning conformation.

"Good breeding shows," she said aloud, repeating an old racing maxim.

Taking care not to disturb the thick wrap on the filly's left leg, Melanie picked out her hooves and ran a soft cloth over her gleaming black coat. Then she gently massaged Image all over. She smiled as she saw the filly drop her head and wriggle her lips, a sign she was enjoying the session in spite of her artificially dulled state.

Leading Image out into the rosy dawn, Melanie paused at a patch of bluegrass just outside the rehabilitation barn. The filly lowered her head and nibbled on a few blades, but then brought her head up and gazed quietly at the training oval.

"I'm sorry, sweetie," Melanie said, feeling as if someone had kicked her in the stomach. "You won't be racing anymore, but we're going to make you into a first-class broodmare. And with any luck, your baby will be out there one day, running its heart out for us both. What do you think of that?"

That seemed to satisfy the filly somehow, and she turned away from the oval. She tugged at her lead, impatient to find the next perfect patch of grass. Melanie started walking, and Image followed, apparently enjoying the warmth of the morning sun.

"Of course, it's going to take some time before your baby will be ready for the track," Melanie babbled while she walked alongside her beloved horse. "So in the meantime I'm going to find another horse to race. And I don't want you to be jealous or anything. We both know who's number one, right?"

Image whuffled Melanie's hair, and Melanie smiled in spite of the sadness that engulfed her whenever she thought of Image's abbreviated racing career.

"And the next thing I need to do is to make arrangements to have you moved to Whitebrook," Melanie said. "It was very cool of Brad to let you come here, but it's time to go home, don't you think?"

Image bobbed her head, almost as if she understood.

Pausing to let Image rest, Melanie let her mind drift lazily to the previous night's party. She scowled as she considered how she'd missed her chance to talk with Harv about riding for him. But soon she replayed the conversation she'd overheard about Flag's Up Farm and the owner who was selling everything, including his stock. "Good bloodlines," the man talking to Brad had said. *Seabiscuit.* Melanie narrowed her eyes as she thought about how quickly Brad had dismissed the subject. She knew that if there were any deals to be had, Brad would be first in line, no matter how much he boasted about not having any interest. Still, Melanie reasoned, he really *did* have a stableful of winning horses. Even though he was bragging, that didn't make his statement less true.

I'll just drive out to the sale this morning, she decided. But then she remembered that Jazz had planned to wait till the fall auctions.

"Just a look, that's all," Melanie said aloud, as if Jazz were right there to challenge her.

Two hours later Melanie was behind the wheel of her Blazer, rattling down the road toward Flag's Up Farm. As she approached the farm, she saw several signs pointing the way to the dispersal sale. Colorful balloons bobbed in bunches on the posts.

It looks like a used-car lot, Melanie thought as she pulled into the long, tree-lined driveway. She fell in line behind a number of trucks and rigs. A bored young guy wearing a frayed shirt waved them toward the stable area. Melanie parked next to a big rig near one of several big green-and-white stable buildings.

Climbing out of the car, Melanie saw several people milling around outside the barns. Some people carried armloads of tack and equipment. Others viewed yearlings that had been led out to small grass paddocks. People crowded along the white fence rails, studying the yearlings' movements intently.

This whole thing looks like a carnival—or a swap meet, Melanie thought. Spotting another young guy wearing the Flag's Up Farm uniform, she made her way over to him.

"I've come to look at your horses," she announced.

The guy looked harried. "You and everyone else in the state of Kentucky," he grumbled, reaching for a halter and lead rope someone had carelessly tossed over a wheelbarrow. "The minute the word's out that someone's business is in trouble, everyone turns up looking for a bargain." He gave Melanie a look of disdain.

"I didn't come for a bargain," declared Melanie hotly. "I came because I heard your farm had some nice bloodstock."

The guy's face softened at the compliment. "Sorry, I don't mean to be a jerk. But this is pretty hard on all of us who work here," he said, giving Melanie a weak smile. "We do have a few nice horses left. I have to show some broodmares to some buyers right now, but if you want to walk around, you're welcome to look. Everything's for sale—everything."

With that, he walked away. Melanie shook her head. It was unbelievably sad. She could just imagine how awful it would be if something happened to Whitebrook and her aunt and uncle were forced to sell everything like this.

Wandering down a barn aisle, Melanie looked sadly at empty stall after empty stall. The doors were

47

thrown open, and she had momentary glimpses of desolate boxes, swept empty till there were only bare floors. No whiskery faces poked through the open doors, no shrill whinnies filled the interior of the barn. Everywhere she looked, there were only signs of a once vibrant establishment.

"Guess they must have already sold the Seabiscuit horse. This is so depressing," Melanie murmured under her breath. She hurried out of the barn and strolled along next to a white fence. She gazed at empty pastures, now overgrown with tall grass. Every so often she spotted a clump of people haggling over a hotwalker or over a couple of mares with foals. Each time, a lump formed in her throat.

Finally Melanie turned past an outbuilding and walked over to a medium-size paddock. She wasn't exactly sure why she just didn't turn around and go home. At the far end of the paddock Melanie spied a thick clump of trees. Peering closer, she saw a massive chestnut colt, his great neck arched in a way that displayed a slight crest. Intrigued, she walked up next to the colt so she could get a better look.

His coat was scraggly, as if he hadn't been groomed for weeks, Melanie noted. Frowning, she noticed that the part of his mane that wasn't sticking up was flopped over to the right side instead of the customary left. *Uh-oh, bad luck*, she thought. The racing world was filled with superstition. Grooms spent long hours training their horses' manes over to the left just to avoid the bad luck that they were sure came with a mane that fell to the wrong side.

This colt has a nice blaze. A two-year-old, Melanie guessed, judging by his long legs and lanky frame. She could see powerful muscles rippling through his hindquarters. He reminded her of another horse, but for the moment she couldn't quite place who that horse was.

The colt threw up his head at her approach and studied her for a moment before lowering his muzzle into a water bucket. He blew into the water and splattered spray around him.

"You're a pretty playful guy, huh?" Melanie said, leaning against the rail. She laughed as the colt nudged the bucket again and again till the clip broke away from the post. The bucket fell into the tall grass. The colt wheeled back at the sudden movement, turning to run from his imagined enemy. His tail flagged and mane flying, he tore around the small paddock several times, neighing shrilly.

"All that ruckus over a little bucket? Aren't you a little old to be getting worked up like this?" Melanie scolded him. She continued admiring him. His big stride was evident even in the confines of the paddock.

After running for a few seconds, the colt stopped

abruptly, planting his front feet and sliding his huge hindquarters under him, sending up dirt clods.

"Ooh, easy on those legs, big guy," Melanie exclaimed, wincing. She pictured his thousand-plus pounds exerting force on those relatively thin, long legs.

Seconds later the chestnut tentatively walked back over to the bucket, nudging it and apparently satisfying himself that it wasn't going to hurt him. Then he turned toward Melanie. Girl and horse stood regarding each other for several minutes.

"You sure are beautiful," Melanie breathed. "I wonder why you're over here all by yourself and not being paraded around to some of those horse-hungry buyers over there."

She couldn't stop staring at the big colt. There was something commanding about him, something about the set of his wide, intelligent eyes and his proud stance. She held out her fingers and wiggled them, enticing him to come over, but he stood stock-still, feet planted squarely, a challenging look on his face.

"Not so friendly, huh?" Melanie said, aching to touch his powerful, sloping shoulder. Without thinking, she bent over and slipped between the rails into the paddock. Of course she knew how foolish it was, climbing into a paddock with a strange horse, especially a colt. And she didn't have permission. Just because the handler had told her to look around, she knew he didn't mean she could have free rein to handle every horse on the place by herself.

Oh, what does it matter? Melanie thought. *I'm not hurting anybody. Just making friends with a lonely horse.*

With a quick motion Melanie reached up to his rough mane and pulled some pieces of straw out. Then she stood back, enjoying the feeling of the sun on her back and the camaraderie of the big, handsome chestnut colt.

"You remind me of someone," Melanie murmured. "You're from some famous line. Wait, it's coming to me—"

Suddenly the colt flattened his ears and lunged straight at her. Melanie jumped back just as someone called, "Hey, what are you doing in there? Are you crazy?"

Melanie whirled around to see the handler she'd talked to earlier break away from a stable hand. He walked toward her and broke into a run. He waved his arms wildly. "Get out of there, *now!*" he shouted.

Scrambling between the rails, Melanie climbed out of the paddock and watched as the colt snaked toward her, eyes pinched shut, his jaws opened wide. His teeth crunched on air as he gave her a menacing look.

"Whoa, what was that all about?" Melanie exclaimed, surprised by the colt's sudden assault.

"I can see you've never been around a horse farm before!" the handler exclaimed.

"What are you talking about?" Melanie snapped. "I've been around horses practically all my life."

"Well, with all that experience, don't you know you're not supposed to get into a paddock with a horse you don't know?" The guy looked at her as if she were a little kid.

"Oh, relax," Melanie said, tossing her head. "It was no big deal."

The handler and the guy he was with looked at each other. "For your information, High Jinx here is an incredibly dangerous horse," the first guy said.

"I'll be glad when Mr. Maynard unloads this one, that's for sure," the other guy said. "He tried to take a chunk out of me this morning."

"So he's for sale?" Melanie asked, watching curiously as the two men started toward the colt. One of them carried a whip and the other a stud chain attached to a lead rope.

"Yep," the handler she'd talked to before said. "A two-year-old with two races to his name. And one of them a claimer. We're about to show him to some small-town sucker and his wife."

The two guys laughed.

"What's wrong with him? Is he lame? Is he sick? Is he a dog on the track?"

The handler shook his head. "None of the above. He's a looker, all right. But you'd better not take your eyes off him for a minute."

"What's that supposed to mean?" Melanie demanded.

"He's a typical Hastings horse," the handler said. "Hastings was Man o' War's grandsire, you know, and he was as mean as a snake. He passed on some of that nasty temper to Fair Play, Man o' War's sire. Man o' War's progeny are pretty notorious for having some real hot blood—and that includes this colt's ancestor, Seabiscuit. This colt seems to have gotten a double helping."

"So this is the horse with the Seabiscuit lines!" Melanie exclaimed, looking at the colt intently.

"Yeah, though when it comes to looks, he's more a throwback to Man o' War," the handler replied.

"Can he run?" Melanie asked simply.

The guy nodded. "Yeah, when he wants to—which is not too often."

"Get over here and help me, Jason, and stop jawing with the girl," the other guy snapped.

Melanie put her hands on her hips, a retort ready to spring to her lips. But then she paused, unnerved by the scene taking place in front of her. As the two guys drew closer to the paddock, the colt pawed the ground menacingly. When they entered the enclosure, the colt wheeled and bolted. It was clear that he didn't like the handlers at all—and it was obvious that he had no intention of being caught. When they closed in on him, he lashed out, first at one handler and then at the other. The colt shook his head and whirled around, raising his front legs threateningly like a horse in battle.

"Knock it off," snarled Jason, slapping at the colt's flanks with the rope.

"You're handling him too roughly," Melanie called out, the words bursting from her involuntarily.

Jason rolled his eyes. "Will you listen to her?" he said mockingly to his friend. "She thinks we're being too rough on our ferocious friend Jinx here."

The other guy laughed coldly but made no reply as he saw his opportunity. The colt stood still and looked as if he'd decided that the game was over. With a lightning move the handler slipped on the halter, pulling the stud chain quickly over the chestnut's nose. "There, you miserable hunk of horseflesh," he muttered, jerking the chain for good measure.

"Where are you taking him?" Melanie called as he led the colt toward the gate.

"To his new home, I hope," he yelled over his shoulder just before the colt skittered sideways, stepping soundly on his foot. "Gilbert, get over here and help me before this horse kills me."

You'd deserve it, Melanie thought harshly, watching

the handlers jostle the colt between them all the way up the hill.

Sighing as the colt disappeared behind a building, Melanie turned toward the other paddocks. Several were empty and overgrown. Only one still housed a couple of yearlings that cavorted through the grass. Although they showed breeding and promise, neither really captured Melanie's imagination, and after a while she wandered on aimlessly.

"I should have gotten here yesterday before all the good horses were sold, I guess," Melanie murmured. Spying another stable building, she walked toward it, hoping that maybe there was a horse or two left that were worth looking at. Again, though, most of the stalls were empty. The three youngsters stabled there didn't strike her as remarkable. Melanie sighed as she passed a girl in her twenties who was pushing a muck cart through the door.

"Is this all the stock you have left?" she asked the girl.

"Pretty much. But you might want to go out on the track," the stable hand replied. "They just brought out a couple of two-year-olds that you might be interested in."

"Thanks," Melanie replied. She made her way over to the training oval, where off in the distance she could see several horses galloping around the far turn. Finding a place on the rail next to an older couple who watched the runners with binoculars, Melanie squinted in the bright sunshine. She studied the horses running down the track. Immediately she spotted the chestnut colt among them. He was bumping against his fellow horses, running with a furious if inconsistent stride. In spite of the fact that he seemed to be going more sideways than forward, he began to move ahead of the pack. But suddenly, as he gained on the front-runner, a gray, he reached over to take a vicious bite.

"A biter," said the man next to Melanie, putting down his binoculars. "So much for that one. We can't have a horse in our barn who tries to eat the competition."

"But look how fast he's running," exclaimed his wife, reaching for the binoculars. "He's blowing their doors off."

Melanie's breath caught in her throat as the colt tore down the track, bucking and kicking out, sending dirt clods flying and leaving the pack behind.

"Doesn't matter," the man replied sourly. "I've heard about this colt, and from what I'm seeing, everything they say is true. He ought to be put down to save everyone the trouble."

Melanie cupped her hand over her face to shield her eyes from the sun as she watched the colt plunge down the track, darting and swerving. All the while, his jockey was fighting with him, whipping him from behind.

"Lay off the whip, you big brute," Melanie growled under her breath, infuriated.

She bit her lip as the colt veered over to the rail.

"He's trying to shed his rider!" exclaimed the woman in Melanie's ear. "I think you're right, dear. We're better off without this one."

The man signaled to the handler that he'd seen enough, and he and his wife turned and walked toward their car.

Melanie sucked in her breath as the jockey managed to slow the colt and jumped off. He narrowly missed being stomped as the big animal reared, plunged, and whirled. Somehow the jockey managed to hang on to the reins until two outriders rode up on either side of the exploding colt.

"Well, he's beautiful, that's for sure. Too bad he hasn't had as much training as he ought to for a two-year-old," Melanie said, turning away.

Though her heart went out to the chestnut and she bridled at the way he was mistreated, she knew better than to consider him any longer.

Image had been untrained when Melanie first laid eyes on her. And she definitely was a handful. But Jinx was another story altogether. Where Image had never been mean, Jinx obviously came dangerously close.

"Forget about him, Graham," Melanie said to herself, walking quickly back to her car. "Talk about complicated. He's definitely not the horse you're looking for."

5

THAT NIGHT MELANIE AWOKE WITH A START. FOR A MOMENT she couldn't remember where she was. All she knew was that she was agitated, tangled up in her thick comforter with her pillow pushed onto the floor. Slowly she became aware that she had been dreaming about a fiery chestnut horse rearing, plunging, and venting his rage.

As the silhouette of the Victorian bedroom she was staying in swam into view, Melanie became aware that she was at Townsend Acres. She realized that the horse she'd been dreaming about was Jinx, the willful colt she had seen that morning.

Her heart pounded, and her throat was parched. Melanie flipped on the light by her bed. She threw

59

back the comforter and padded over to the kitchen area to get a drink of water.

How weird is that? she thought. *Me, dreaming.* Since her days were physically demanding, she usually fell into a deep, dreamless sleep at night. And on the rare occasion that she did have dreams, she rarely had any about horses. This night, however, was a different story. While she sipped from her glass she gazed out at the rehabilitation barn, which was bathed in moonlight, and tried to calm herself. But it didn't work. She couldn't stop shaking, and she couldn't stop thinking about Jinx.

What is it about that colt? Melanie wondered, pushing back her tousled blond hair. He was beautiful, all right. But so were lots of other horses. And he had superb bloodlines, but once again, so did lots of other horses.

He has it, Melanie suddenly realized. That pull, that final ingredient, that magic she'd been looking for that would bind their hearts together and make them a perfect racing partnership. It was the same thing that had drawn her to Image when she'd first encountered the filly at Vince Jones's training barn two years earlier at Turfway Park.

"You're losing it, Graham," she told herself, swallowing the last of the water. "You want a new horse so much, you're twisting it around in your head so that he fits."

But what if he does fit? she challenged herself.

For the next few hours Melanie sat huddled in a chair with her arms wrapped around her feet. Mentally she reviewed everything she'd seen and heard about Jinx. She couldn't seem to arrive at a clear-cut conclusion. Finally she took a deep breath.

Maybe I should just stop trying to reason it out so much. Sometimes a girl's just got to follow her heart, she told herself decisively.

Of course, she didn't have the money to buy Jinx by herself. Even if his owner would sell the unruly colt cheaply just to get rid of him, she'd have to call Jazz and have him wire her the money. And maybe she ought to ask her aunt and uncle, Ashleigh Griffen and Mike Reese, to come with her to the farm to get their opinion. It wasn't that Melanie didn't feel confident of her ability to judge a horse for soundness and racing potential, but it wouldn't hurt to have an expert second opinion as well. She dismissed the thought. Maybe just this once it would be better not to get a second opinion. She had a feeling her aunt would tell her "No way."

"Here goes nothing," Melanie finally muttered. She had no idea what time it was in France. But suddenly that didn't matter. All that mattered was to convince Jazz that this was the horse and that they'd better act quickly if they didn't want the colt to get away. For all she knew, Jinx could have been sold after she'd left Flag's Up Farm that afternoon; he might already be on his way to his new home.

Breathlessly she waited after she punched in the number of Jazz's hotel room.

"Hello?" Jazz's voice sounded thick with sleep.

"Jazz, it's Melanie. I hope I didn't wake you up," Melanie said apologetically, though she knew she probably had.

"Uh, it's after ten here, so I ought to be up, but we had a late night last night. Are you okay?"

Melanie gripped the phone. "I'm okay," she said in a rush. "But I've found a horse."

"A what?"

"A horse," Melanie repeated.

"That sure was quick," Jazz replied. "Are you sure you aren't being impulsive? I thought we were going to wait and go together to the fall auctions."

"Yeah, I know!" Melanie exclaimed impatiently. "But it just kinda happened. There's this farm at the edge of town and I'd heard that the owner's selling out, so I dropped by. And oh, Jazz, you wouldn't believe this colt. Man o' War bloodlines. He's stunning. He's fast. He's perfect."

"Perfect?"

Melanie could hear Jazz's disbelief. Closing her eyes, she pictured Jinx trying to stomp his groom.

Then she thought about his performance on the track and how he'd worked furiously to spread his rider out like butter along the rail.

"Well, not perfect, exactly," she confessed. "But close."

"Close, huh?" Jazz said skeptically. "Exactly what's not perfect about him?"

Melanie hesitated. "He's uh, got a bit of a bad temper." Guiltily she wondered if the words "bad temper" were strong enough.

"*Bad* bad temper?" Jazz nudged. "Or just . . . bad temper?"

"Bad, bad temper," Melanie confessed. "But redeemable. Fixable."

"Nuh-uh, Mel," Jazz fired back. "Remember? We said that this time we were sticking with a horse with an uncomplicated personality."

"I know, I know," Melanie rushed in. "But you've got to see this horse, and then you'll fall in love with him just like I did."

"Melanie, you know I don't know that much about racehorses," Jazz went on. "But I do know a little something about Man o' War. Even those of us who aren't horse-racing addicts read horse books when we were kids. And everyone's heard about Man o' War's famous temper. 'The mostest hoss that ever was'— wasn't that what his groom said? He probably meant it as a compliment, but it also says something else about him. He was a whole lotta horse in every way. I'd say we're better off passing him up."

"You don't understand, Jazz!" Melanie exclaimed. "He's got some issues, that's for sure. But I don't think it's all genetics. I mean, you should have seen how his handlers were treating him. And his jockey—he ought to find a new job. He has no business being around horses. No wonder poor Jinx is a head case!"

Jazz was quiet for a moment. "Well, I haven't heard you worked up about a horse like this before, Graham. That is, except for Image." He took a deep breath, and Melanie could hear him slowly exhale.

He's gonna go for it, she thought, feeling her heart race.

"He's sound, right?" Jazz asked, suddenly all business.

"Yep, I looked him over myself, every inch." Melanie was uncomfortably aware that what she'd said wasn't quite truthful. She hadn't been able to get close enough to touch him, let alone examine him. "Of course, I'll look over the vet reports before signing the deal."

"Can we afford him?" Jazz went on.

"Normally we couldn't," Melanie replied. "But his owner's close to bankruptcy and dispersing everything. I know he'll be reasonable."

"You really feel it in your heart? This is the horse?" Jazz said.

"I know it," Melanie said. "He's been haunting me for hours. It's meant to be."

Jazz was silent for so long, Melanie wondered if the phone connection had been broken. Finally she heard him laugh.

"Graham, if you decide not to become a jockey after all, you ought to become a salesperson. You're absolutely relentless. I can't believe I'm cracking!" he exclaimed.

Melanie grinned so widely, her face hurt. "You mean we can do it?"

"Why not? After all, racing is about risking everything, right?" Jazz said, chuckling at her enthusiasm.

"He's going to be great, Jazz, you'll see!" Melanie replied.

She and Jazz agreed on the top price they were willing to pay, and after Melanie hung up, she sat hugging herself, waiting impatiently for daybreak.

Before first light Melanie threw on her clothes and darted down to Image's stall to check on her. A few minutes later she was on her way to Whitebrook, where she ducked into the barn office. Ashleigh was sitting by the phone, nervously flicking her ponytail while she flipped through some papers. She looked up when Melanie entered, and Melanie could tell by her face that something was seriously wrong.

"What is it, Aunt Ashleigh?"

Ashleigh let out a deep sigh. "One of the brood-mares colicked badly during the night, and Dani and I have been taking turns walking her. Dr. Seymour's supposed to call any minute."

"That's terrible. Can I help in any way?" Melanie asked automatically, but Ashleigh shook her head.

Feeling embarrassed, considering her aunt's worry over the colicking mare, Melanie nevertheless plunged in and asked to borrow Whitebrook's rig.

"What for, Melanie?" Ashleigh said, eyeing her curiously.

"I think I've found a horse!" Melanie exclaimed. "Is there room in the training barn? I'll give you the details later. If I don't move now, I might lose him."

Ashleigh frowned as she pulled her keys out of her pocket, and Melanie was afraid that she'd insist on coming with her. But just then the phone rang. Before Ashleigh spoke to the caller, she covered the mouth-piece with her hand and asked Melanie, "Do you want Joe to go with you to help with loading?"

Joe Kisner was one of Whitebrook's grooms, and he often hauled the Whitebrook horses.

Melanie started to say it wasn't necessary, but then,

remembering the way Jinx had exploded with his handlers, she changed her mind. *Better safe than sorry*, she thought.

"Can you spare him for a little while?"

"Sure," Ashleigh replied.

Melanie scampered toward the training barn, hoping that Joe would be free to leave right away. She didn't have any more time to lose. Someone could be stopping by the unfortunate farm that very moment to clean out the last of its stock. Maybe there was someone else out there who was as crazy as she was and willing to take a chance on a beautiful bad boy.

"Big day, huh?" Joe said as he expertly swung the rig onto the highway a few minutes later.

Melanie, who sat on the edge of the seat in the cab, nodded vigorously. "Absolutely," she said, grinning from ear to ear.

They arrived at Flag's Up Farm, and Melanie hurried back to the colt's paddock while Joe parked the rig. She saw that Jinx was still grazing in the enclosure.

Just the way I remember him, Melanie thought, her heart catching in her throat at his beauty and imperiousness.

Looking around, Melanie finally located Gilbert coming out of a barn with an empty feed cart. Patting the checkbook in her pocket, she headed toward Gilbert and asked him where she could find Mr. Maynard. "I want to buy one of his horses," she said.

Gilbert gave her a knowing look. Then he shook his head. "It's none of my business how you rich girls spend your money," he said.

"I'm not a rich girl," Melanie tossed back, insulted.

But Gilbert went on. "If you're considering who I think you are, as his groom, I gotta tell you, I'd think twice about it. Particularly if you enjoy the feeling of your head sitting where it's supposed to be, between your shoulders. "

"I know what I'm doing," Melanie retorted, annoyed at Gilbert's interference.

"Well, it's been nice knowin' ya," Gilbert said with a shrug, leading the way toward the barn office.

An hour later Melanie emerged from Richard Maynard's office clutching a transfer of ownership and a vet report. When she approached Joe, who was leaning against the rig sipping from a coffee cup, she resisted the urge to wave the paper.

"Got High Jinx for a song!" she crowed. Though she and Jazz had agreed upon a price, she was pleasantly surprised at how quickly Maynard had settled on a much lower amount.

"Good for you," Joe replied, clapping her on the shoulder. "Now let's go see this next winner of yours!"

Melanie practically skipped all the way to the paddock. Gilbert, she saw, had haltered Jinx and had his stud chain firmly wrapped over his nose. Once again he had enlisted help, this time a tall, burly man who looked as though he didn't take any guff from anyone. He reminded Melanie of some of the bouncers she'd seen at some of the rowdy concerts she went to in New York and around Lexington.

"This is Big Al," Gilbert said, motioning to the big man. "He'll help us load this live wire."

"Oh, Melanie and I can handle it ourselves," Joe said airily.

Big Al shook his head and reached for the colt's lead rope, gripping it tightly and eyeing him warily.

"Don't you pull any of your shenanigans, Jinx, you hear?" he said to the big red colt.

"First thing we're going to do when we get you home is groom you," Melanie said softly, eyeing her new purchase with pride.

"Good luck," Big Al growled. Gilbert opened the gate, and the two led the huge colt out toward the stable area.

"I'll get his shipping bandages," Melanie said, scooting ahead toward the rig.

"Don't bother," Gilbert called out.

Melanie stopped and looked back, ready to contradict Gilbert. Instead her words caught in her throat as

Jinx pulled his head up, practically lifting Big Al off his feet.

"None of your nonsense," Big Al exclaimed, letting loose with a stream of bad words.

"I'll take him," Joe said, reaching over for the lead rope.

Big Al stepped deftly out of the way and continued leading Jinx toward the rig. Joe opened the back doors and let down the big rubber-coated ramps just as Jinx planted his hooves and refused to budge.

Melanie and Joe stood watching as Big Al and Gilbert cajoled, threatened, and finally bribed Jinx with carrots.

"Come on, big guy," Melanie cooed into his ear. "You'll love Whitebrook, I promise."

Jinx flattened his ears at Melanie and lunged toward her, causing her to leap back.

"I'll take over now," Joe finally said, firmly taking the lead from Big Al.

Clucking softly to the chestnut colt, Joe gently urged him forward. Jinx stopped dead and looked menacingly at Joe. Suddenly he plunged up the ramp as if someone had set fire to his tail.

6

MELANIE CLOSED THE TRAILER DOOR AS SOON AS JINX WAS inside, and waited anxiously for Joe to come out.

"Whew! Done! And I'm alive to tell about it," Joe said, emerging a few seconds later from the front compartment.

"Good!" Melanie exclaimed with relief.

"Good riddance!" Big Al muttered.

"You can say that again," Gilbert chimed in. Taking off his sweaty cap, he waved at Melanie. "Good luck. You're going to need every bit of it."

Melanie smirked at the handler as she climbed into the cab. "I'm sure we'll be just fine," she called out. Turning to Joe, she added, "Let's get out of here. This poor horse has had enough of this place!"

Joe scratched the stubble on his chin. He frowned as Jinx kicked against the walls of the rig. Starting up the engine, Joe pulled up the long driveway and headed out onto the highway.

"Crazy horse is going to punch a hole through if he doesn't calm down," the groom said.

Melanie swallowed hard and tried to ignore the horrific din coming from the back of the rig. All the way back to Whitebrook Jinx kicked and threw himself against the walls. By the time they turned into the driveway, Melanie was perspiring so much from nerves, her armpits were soaked.

"Hasn't gotten much training, has he," commented Joe dryly while he set the brake and climbed out of the cab.

"This poor horse hasn't gotten much of anything," Melanie replied, scrambling out of the cab and hurrying toward the back to let down the ramp. "I intend to change all that—starting now."

The minute she lowered the ramp and Joe backed the colt down the incline, she saw that Jinx had worked himself up into a lather.

He looks terrified, Melanie thought, her heart going out to the colt. Had he been in a trailer accident before? she wondered briefly. Jinx suddenly snaked out his head and tried to take a bite out of Joe's shoulder.

"No, you don't," Joe yelped, leaping out of the way of the horse's powerful jaws.

"Did he get you?" asked Melanie anxiously.

Joe shook his head. "No, but not for lack of trying," he muttered. "I'm beginning to think Big Al wasn't just being a grouch about this horse."

Since it was after morning works and just before lunch, things were quiet at Whitebrook. The stable yard was deserted.

Good thing no one's around to see the way Jinx is behaving. I wouldn't want anyone to get the wrong impression, Melanie thought.

Eyeing his new surroundings, Jinx snorted and pawed the earth. He arched his neck and let loose with a trumpeting neigh that shook his entire body.

"He's announcing himself," Melanie crowed delightedly, trying to cover up how nervous she felt about the way Jinx had just gone after Joe.

"I think he announced himself with that bite," Joe muttered, keeping a watchful eye on Jinx.

Melanie walked ahead as Joe led Jinx to an empty stall in the training barn, one several doors down from where Star, Christina's horse, was housed. Taking the lead from Joe, she maneuvered the big horse into his new home.

"Check it out. Big, roomy stall. Lots of thick bedding," Melanie remarked as the big horse sniffed the stall walls suspiciously. She led him over to the automatic waterer, but Jinx didn't appear to want to drink. After she unbuckled Jinx's halter, Melanie stepped out and closed the door, peering in through the bars.

Immediately Jinx began pacing in his stall. He walked round and round the interior, cutting a circular path through his bedding.

"Hope he settles in soon," Joe said before walking off.

"Oh, he will. He just has to get used to his new home," Melanie replied. She stayed, standing back from the stall but close enough to observe the colt. She wanted to pinch herself. She couldn't believe this beautiful, spirited horse was hers.

"I have big plans for you," Melanie told Jinx happily. For a moment she lost herself in a daydream of piloting the big red horse down the track at Keeneland, picturing him far out front, his legs pumping like pistons.

"And he's ahead by a length, now two, now another in a blistering display of speed!" An imaginary announcer's voice rang in Melanie's head, and she grinned like an idiot.

"Hey, is that your new horse?" called out Dani Martens, Star's groom, who was leading a bay filly down the barn aisle.

Melanie was about to answer when Jinx lunged savagely at the stall door, teeth bared and ears pinned. Only the metal bars stopped him, and the stall door shuddered with the tremendous impact of his body. The filly Dani had been leading shied and leaped side-ways, her hooves ringing in the barn aisle. Jinx ran his teeth back and forth along the bars, creating a scraping noise that made Melanie's ears hurt. The colt was plainly determined to get at the filly.

"Yikes," Dani said, abruptly turning the filly in the opposite direction. "Not much in the manners depart-ment, is he?"

"Oh, he just needs a little time," Melanie replied sharply. She knew she sounded defensive, but she couldn't help it.

Turning back toward Jinx, she talked to him calmly and was pleased when he stopped raking his teeth on the bars. "Forget the grooming for now. Maybe I'll just leave you alone for a while so you can get used to your new home, okay, Jinx?"

Jinx responded by turning his massive quarters toward her and kicking out, his hoof making loud con-tact with the wall.

That evening, as soon as she returned to Townsend Acres, Melanie called her father. He had just returned

75

to New York with his wife, Susan. Melanie was eager to share her exciting news.

"Guess what?" she said when Will answered the phone. Without waiting for him to guess, she told him all about her new horse. She didn't go into great detail about Jinx's temperament, but she could tell her dad's antennae went up when she called the chestnut "spirited."

"'Spirited'?" Will repeated. "What do you mean by that?"

Quickly Melanie backpedaled a little. "Oh, you know. Just young. Typical racehorse. Well, maybe more than a typical racehorse." She frowned, trying to find the right words without outright lying. "He has a few issues, like biting and kicking. It's nothing that can't be managed with some proper training."

She heard her father sigh deeply. "Out with it, Mel. What have you gotten yourself into?"

"Oh, Dad," Melanie said, exasperated. "You don't have to go into worry mode, okay? I've done this before. And look how well Image turned out!"

"Not before she gave your dear old dad a few new gray hairs," Will replied sternly. "Image was spirited, but from what you're telling me, this colt sounds like something more."

Everyone's so quick to write Jinx off, Melanie thought furiously, staring out at the night sky for a long time

76

after she hung up with her dad. She was tempted to wish on the first star she saw that Jinx would stop clowning around and start realizing some of the potential she was sure he had.

That's a lot of wish for one poor little star to handle. Probably wouldn't help a bit, she thought, turning away from the window. *I've just got to work hard with him, the way I did with Image.*

As Melanie got ready to doze off, she mentally reviewed all the things she had done to bring out the best in Image, in spite of her willful ways.

I'll just use the same recipe on this horse, Melanie thought, closing her eyes. *Lots of love, lots of attention, and lots of sweat.*

The minute Melanie drove onto the grounds at White-brook the next morning, she sensed that something was wrong. Her suspicions were confirmed when she hurried into the training barn and saw Joe nailing planks up against Jinx's stall. The wall facing the barn aisle looked as though someone had blown a hole in it with a stick of dynamite.

"What happened?" she cried, rushing over.

Joe, whose mouth was full of nails, mumbled a reply that Melanie couldn't understand. The most she could make out were the words "pain in the rear."

"Where's Jinx?"

Joe pointed toward the paddock area, and Melanie tore down the aisle, relaxing only when she saw Jinx standing in one of the smaller paddocks, eating grass and looking as if he didn't have a care in the world.

"What have you done now, you great big doof?" Melanie scolded the big colt, barely masking her relief.

"What *hasn't* he done?" grumbled Joe, coming up behind her, toolbox in hand. "He kept me awake all night with his racket, and he kept every horse at Whitebrook awake as well. Whinnying, pacing, kicking, carrying on . . ."

"He must be missing his home at Flag's Up," Melanie responded, reaching out her palm as the colt sniffed the air suspiciously.

"He's missing a few marbles in his head," Joe replied sourly. "I brought him his breakfast, and he decided he didn't want to wait. He turned around and tried to kick his stall down so he could get at his food."

"He likes his feed, so what?" Melanie blurted out, placing her hands on her hips.

Joe gave her a long look before setting off with his toolbox.

"High Jinx, you're not making friends around here," Melanie said softly as she turned back to the chestnut.

Jinx pawed the ground, then walked away from her, standing in the middle of his paddock and glaring at the world.

"This pretty boy is a real handful," Ashleigh remarked that afternoon when Melanie returned to Whitebrook to look in on Jinx after she'd taken Image for her daily swim in the Townsend Acres therapy pool.

"He is, isn't he?" Melanie said proudly. She examined the chestnut standing squarely in the sun, his head lifted regally.

"I didn't exactly mean that as a compliment," Ashleigh said quietly. "Joe has flatly refused to give Jinx his feed, and he's never done that before. I asked Dani to take over, and she agreed to do it, so at least that's taken care of."

Melanie hung her head. "I'm sorry if he's causing problems, Aunt Ashleigh," she said. "But I promise I'll work with him, and I'll get him sorted out right away."

Ashleigh laid a hand on her shoulder. "I believe you will, but in the meantime you need to take it very slowly with this horse. You also need to be extra careful around him. I don't want you getting hurt."

Though Melanie knew her aunt was only concerned for her safety, she couldn't help feeling annoyed that Ashleigh was sounding just like her dad. She was being overprotective. Jinx just had a few kinks to work out. That was all.

Melanie spent the rest of the afternoon hanging around Jinx's paddock, watching him intently. She wanted to memorize his every movement. She thought that if she studied him enough, she might learn something about the colt that could help her understand the reason for his bad behavior.

But as she headed back to Townsend Acres that evening, Melanie felt that she hadn't learned much of anything except how much it hurt to have Jinx ram his head against her because she dared to get too close.

"He didn't mean it," she told Jazz when he rang late that night and she told him about Jinx and his latest escapades.

"I'm sure you'll figure him out, Graham," Jazz said loyally. Melanie didn't like the sound of doubt in his voice. Still, she decided, once he was finished with his tour and could come to Whitebrook and see Jinx for himself, he'd see what a winner the colt was.

If I can just keep Jinx out of trouble till then, Melanie thought grimly.

7

THE NEXT DAY MELANIE TRIED UNSUCCESSFULLY TO GROOM Jinx. Though he didn't object too much when she haltered him and took him to the crossties, he lashed out like an animal possessed when she picked up a rubber currycomb. When Melanie tried to run the comb over his rough coat, he cow-kicked and hurled himself sideways.

"Easy there, big guy," Melanie crooned softly. She stood talking to him for a long time before making another attempt, but Jinx still refused to let her do much more than touch him. Though he submitted to her hand, the minute she approached with the brush, he'd cock his hind leg warningly.

Ashleigh stopped in the aisle and watched Melanie's repeated attempts to brush him. "It's obvious that he's been handled," she said. "But he sure doesn't like it, does he?"

Melanie shook her head. "He's definitely got a mind of his own."

"When do you leave for Belmont?" Ashleigh asked, changing the subject.

Melanie bit her lip. "This evening," she said worriedly. She wished Ashleigh hadn't reminded her. She'd be gone for two days, and she needed someone to help care for Jinx while she was gone.

I'd better not ask Aunt Ashleigh, Melanie decided. She knew her aunt had enough on her mind without adding a difficult horse to her problems.

Just then Naomi Traeger, a jockey who rode many of Whitebrook's mounts, came over. While Naomi conferred with Ashleigh about one of the horses in training, Melanie decided to ask her to watch Jinx while she was gone. Naomi was experienced and strong. She'd know how to handle Jinx.

But before she could say anything, Naomi shot her a pointed look, then turned to Ashleigh. "Every horse I rode this morning was a basket case, Ashleigh. They all came out cranky and sluggish—even Star."

"Why is that?" Ashleigh asked.

Naomi looked again at Melanie and then at Jinx. "I hate to say it, but Hex Horse here has been keeping them awake all night, and it doesn't help their performances any to be sleep-deprived."

Melanie was ready to fire off a reply, but she realized that Naomi hadn't spoken anything but the truth.

"He hasn't settled in very well," she admitted.

Guess I can't ask Naomi, she thought. *Jinx definitely hasn't made a very good first impression on her. Now who else can I ask?*

When Naomi and Ashleigh left, Melanie turned back to her colt.

"I'm going to be away for a couple of days, so you've got to be good and not give anyone any trouble," she told Jinx. "When I get back, we're going to get to work and figure out how to get rid of your inner meanie. You can't go around scaring everyone forever."

It was just before evening feeds when Melanie managed to corner Dani.

"I know you don't like Jinx much, but could I ask you a huge favor?" she asked. Seeing Dani's expression, Melanie forged ahead before Dani could refuse. "I'm flying back to Belmont tonight—I'm riding in the Bowling Green. Could you please, please take care of Jinx while I'm gone?"

Dani frowned. "Doing what?"

"Just turn him out, feed him, that's all."

"That's *all*?" Dani repeated. "As if feeding him and

turning him out didn't mean risking life and limb."

"I know he's kind of tough," Melanie admitted. "But I don't have anyone else to care for him."

Dani didn't answer.

"I'll clean all your tack for you for a week," Melanie offered. "C'mon. It's just for two days. I'll be back Sunday."

"Oh, okay," Dani agreed reluctantly. Then she gave Melanie a measured look. "Why do you care about this horse so much, anyway? He couldn't care less about you. In fact, he'd probably enjoy ripping you to ribbons."

Melanie was startled by the question, and she gazed at Jinx. "I don't know how to explain it," she replied truthfully. "I guess it's just because I know deep down he's not the big bad horse he tries to pretend he is."

"Huh," snorted Dani just as Jinx lashed out at Melanie with snapping jaws and a menacing head shake.

Bayleaf had just been loaded in the starting gate for the Bowling Green Handicap on Saturday. Melanie looked down at the colt she was riding while she adjusted her goggles. Listening to the other gates shut, she cleared her throat and thought about the race to come.

"This horse doesn't need a lot of chatter," the

trainer had instructed her beforehand. "He knows his job, and he just needs to be able to do it."

Sounds like a no-brainer, thought Melanie. She was used to dealing with horses that required a great deal of finessing. Still, she decided, she knew better than to think that any racehorse could be set on autopilot. No race was ever a sure thing.

While the track staff continued loading the other horses in the field, Melanie braced herself. She shifted her weight forward and gathered her reins. Glancing quickly to her left, she saw that she and Bayleaf were positioned next to a big chestnut. He reminded her of Jinx.

Please, Jinx, don't kick out any buildings while I'm away, Melanie prayed as she considered her problem horse. Bayleaf danced in the gate, and Melanie forced her mind back to the race at hand. Thinking about other things while racing a Thoroughbred was definitely a good way to get killed, she thought fleetingly.

Turning her gaze to the track ahead of her, Melanie considered the vast expanse. She blocked out the sounds of the spectators jamming the grandstands. It was time to focus on her strategy. She wanted to make a good impression on Andy Chalon, since the trainer had been nice enough to give her a chance to ride for him.

Just then the bell rang and the gate broke open.

Bayleaf poured out of the gate, surging forward.

Go for the rail. Watch for traps. Rate him. Find a hole—then open him up and let him fly! Melanie told herself as she and the colt flew down the track.

Finding her momentum, Melanie studied the field and made her move at the first turn. Pretty soon she found herself in front of the pack. She felt herself fill with exhilaration for a few seconds, till horses began closing in on Bayleaf. Soon they eased around him, but Melanie wasn't worried. She could tell he had plenty of energy in reserve.

Keep the pace, she told herself, enjoying the steady rhythm of Bayleaf's pounding hoofbeats.

The announcer's voice blared out, "Sparkling Effect, Valmont, and Funnyman are in the lead, with Bayleaf and Candoo right on their heels."

Melanie squinted through her splattered goggles at Candoo, the horse who was flanking Bayleaf. He appeared to be flagging slightly.

He'll be out of it soon, Melanie thought. Glancing under her arm to size up the rest of the field, she decided they were still behind enough not to pose a threat. Then Melanie looked up between her horse's ears to gauge the front-runners, who still maintained a slight lead.

Urging Bayleaf forward even faster and putting pressure on one rein, Melanie moved the colt toward the rail. The track rolled out under her at a terrifying speed. The spectators' clothes blurred together in a colorful backdrop as she and the game colt tore on.

Patiently Melanie waited to make her move as she scanned the three horses in front of them, looking for an opening. Finding none, she considered going wide.

Did Bayleaf have it in him to eat more ground and run harder to make it up? Melanie wondered. But soon she realized that she didn't have an option. *I might as well find out.*

"Let's go," Melanie called to her mount, rocking forward even more over his shoulders.

Bayleaf responded by moving out and lengthening his strides. He swept around the three horses that had been in the lead. Several of their jockeys began whipping their mounts. For one unnerving second Melanie wondered if their horses had more in their tanks than Bayleaf. But seconds later Bayleaf pulled ahead, and Melanie grinned as once again she savored the satisfaction of being out in front.

Soon they were flying past the finish, and Melanie stood up in her stirrups. She grinned even wider and patted Bayleaf's sweat-soaked neck.

The roar of the crowd filled the air as Melanie closed her hands slightly on the reins so that the colt would begin to slow.

The outrider who met her to escort her to the winner's circle threw her a congratulatory smile. "Well ridden," he said briefly.

"Picture-perfect," crowed his owner, a funny-looking man in a blinding yellow plaid jacket who was waiting in the circle with Andy Chalon, the trainer.

"Couldn't have been better!" Chalon said, reaching up to shake her hand. "I'll have to have you ride for me again."

When the pictures were taken and Melanie dismounted, she made her way to the jockeys' lounge. Though everyone's praise still rang in her ears, Melanie couldn't help feeling a little unsettled as she cast her thoughts home to Kentucky.

What havoc is Jinx wreaking at Whitebrook? she wondered.

"It's kind of funny," she told Christina that night back at the motel. "I'm more nervous just *thinking* about Jinx than I am actually hurtling along at almost forty miles an hour on a thousand-pound racehorse."

"Some ice princess you are!" Christina joked. But then she furrowed her brow. "Just what kind of a horse *did* you buy, Mel?" she asked worriedly.

You don't want to know, Melanie thought, heading wearily for the bathroom to take a bath. She knew it would take more than a few bubbles to soak away her concerns about her newest problem horse, but it didn't hurt to try.

After landing once again at the airport just outside Lexington on Sunday, Melanie grabbed her bag and rushed out of the terminal toward the parking lot. She'd done this so many times over the last few weeks, she felt as though she could do it in her sleep.

She drove eagerly to Townsend Acres to see Image and spent an hour with her filly, crooning into her ear and telling her about her exciting win at Belmont.

"Bayleaf was the perfect gentleman," Melanie murmured. "But you know what? Riding him only reminded me that I'd rather have an exciting horse like you any day!"

And like Jinx, she added to herself. But soon she felt her stomach lurch at the thought of heading over to Whitebrook. It wasn't that she wasn't dying to see Jinx. It was just that she wasn't sure she was ready to face whatever mess he'd gotten himself into while she'd been gone.

Stop borrowing trouble, Super-Chicken, she commanded herself. She jumped into the Blazer and set off for Whitebrook.

But when she arrived, Melanie knew that once again Jinx had been up to something.

"Want to hear about the equipment that new horse of yours has destroyed?" Mike said by way of greeting when she entered the training barn.

Melanie thought he was joking, but a few minutes later, when she asked Joe what her uncle had been referring to, he rattled off a list: a wheelbarrow, two buckets, and a muck cart. So when she saw Mike out repairing the paddock fence where Jinx was turned out for the morning, she apologized to him.

"I'll replace everything with my winnings," Melanie said quickly.

Mike shook his head. "That's okay," he said, waving away her apology. "Let's just focus on getting that colt under control as soon as possible, shall we?"

Melanie nodded and rushed over to Jinx, anxious to make sure nothing had happened to him while she was gone.

"We're going to get to work, starting tomorrow," Melanie scolded the big colt, who waited in his stall, banging the wall and demanding his feed.

Dani approached with the feed cart. "You're back," she said matter-of-factly to Melanie.

Melanie rushed over to grab the hay from her. "I'll feed him tonight," she said.

"Good!" Dani exclaimed, walking down the aisle.

When Melanie opened the door to the stall, Jinx

immediately crowded her. He raised his hoof and pinned his ears.

"Get back. Stop trying to fool me with your I'm-so-bad act, you goofball," she told him firmly. She pushed her way past and dumped his feed into the bin.

Jinx buried his face in his food while Melanie slipped back out the door.

There. That wasn't hard, she thought, dusting off her jeans. *Dani made a big deal about nothing.*

Then she went in search of Ashleigh.

"I've got to get Jinx on a serious training schedule," Melanie explained to her aunt when she caught up with her in the yearling barn. "No wonder he's so keyed up. He's a racehorse, and he's done nothing but stand around since he's gotten to Whitebrook."

Ashleigh didn't seem to be in any hurry to get him out on the track. "Work him in the round pen. Let's saddle him up a few times before we take him out," she said, much to Melanie's frustration.

"I'm sorry, Melanie," Dani told her on Tuesday just after morning feeds. "That horse of yours tore the sleeve half off my barn jacket this morning. You want him fed, you feed him."

"Sorry, Dani," Melanie said. "He didn't mean to

hurt you. He just needs to learn a little patience. I'll replace your jacket, and I'll take over his feeds."

How am I going to do that when I head back to Belmont and then off to Saratoga? she wondered uneasily. Well, she decided, she'd have to worry about that later. In the meantime she'd better focus on making progress with the unruly colt in the ground-manners department.

Though she'd started trying to groom Jinx from the day she'd brought him home to Whitebrook, she hadn't made much headway. Although he'd finally allowed her to run a brush over his unkempt coat, he still refused to allow her to touch his mane. Each time she toyed with it he jerked angrily against his crossties and thrashed around.

"Maybe he's real sensitive there. Or maybe he had a bad experience with mane-pulling or something. Guess it'll have to wait," Melanie said with a shrug. "I don't need to rush training it to the other side."

Jonnie, another Whitebrook groom, disagreed. "You'd better change that mane right away. It's bad luck," he said, walking past carrying several buckets of supplements.

Jinx stamped his hoof, as if daring anyone to touch his mane.

"I might just keep it the way it is. Too many silly superstitions around the racing world, if you ask me,"

Melanie grumbled, sticking out her tongue at Johnnie's retreating back. So what if she was acting childish? She didn't care. She just wished people would mind their own business!

Melanie finished lunging Jinx. As she put him away she heard the barn phone ring. After a few rings she decided that no one else was going to pick it up, so she did.

"Is that you, Melanie?" It was Christina, calling from Belmont. "When are you coming back here? You're missing all kinds of rides."

"Are you kidding?" Melanie asked. "I did my best when I was there to let everyone know I was available to ride. The best I could do was manage one little mount."

"Vince Jones dropped by today, asking whether you were around, and so did a couple of other trainers," Christina replied.

"Their timing definitely stinks," grumbled Melanie. "Where were they when I was out scrounging rides? Oh, well, I'll be back at Belmont soon."

"Good," said Christina. "Because the meet's ending in a week. Anyway, when you're here, I don't have to worry about what your man-eater is doing to you there."

"Man-eater?" Melanie replied. "Who told you Jinx is a man-eater?"

"Everyone. It's all over the track here," Christina replied. "When you told me the night of the Bowling Green that you were worried about him, I had no idea it was because he had such a bad reputation. I can't believe what I'm hearing."

Melanie stiffened. "What have you heard?" she demanded, suddenly feeling protective of her colt.

"Well, if you really want to know, Mel, I hear that you have a horse and a half," Christina said with a light laugh.

"That's true," Melanie shot back. "Just wait till you see him. He's amazing. His bloodlines go back to Man o' War and Seabiscuit, and he's gorgeous. Chestnut. Really tall. I can't wait to take him out on the track and show everyone around here what he's made of."

Christina paused. "I hear he's a one-horse wrecking crew," she finally said.

"Okay, so he's got a bit of a temper," Melanie confessed. "But he's got a whole lot more. As soon as I get through to him and start working him regularly so that he doesn't have all this pent-up energy, he'll be amazing. Then people won't be so quick to gossip about him."

"Oh, Mel, don't get all tweaked," Christina said quickly. "I know he's going to be great. You've got a good eye for a winner, that's for sure, but I'm still worried."

But Mel still felt she had to convince her cousin. "Seriously, Chris, you ought to have seen him when he went out on the oval at the farm where I bought him. He left all the other horses in the dust once he got going."

"Cool," Christina responded. "But be careful. I have a funny feeling about this horse of yours."

Christina just said that because of what happened to Callie, Melanie thought. *She has funny feelings about almost every horse these days.*

"Hey, Mel, I hate to cut you short, but is my mom there? I need to talk to her about Star," Christina said.

Star, Star, Star, Melanie thought grumpily. She set down the phone and went to look for her aunt, annoyed at how quickly Christina seemed to be dismissing her horse.

After she'd located Ashleigh and told her of Christina's call, Melanie walked toward Jinx's paddock.

"You and I are going to bond, big guy," she said, slipping in between the rails. "We'll show everyone that they're way wrong about you."

Jinx lowered his head and flattened his ears, but Melanie didn't back away. Instead she held out a carrot and called softly to the big colt. Relieved, she saw his ears prick forward with interest. And instead of lunging toward her, he walked over almost eagerly. He picked up his feet with care and reached out with his lips to take the carrot. Then he allowed her to rub his nose while he crunched, letting out a little sigh of pleasure.

See? Melanie thought triumphantly.

It was a small sign of acceptance, but a sign all the same.

8

"She looks as good as she did on race day," called Ralph Dunkirk, Townsend Acres' head trainer, the next morning.

Melanie was walking Image on the soft grass, and she halted as the trainer headed over from the barn.

Ordinarily Melanie wouldn't even speak to Ralph if she could help it. She had never trusted him or liked his methods. But now it didn't seem right to give anyone at Townsend Acres a hard time. She owed them all so much.

"Yes, she does look well, doesn't she?" Melanie replied evenly. She reached over to stroke Image's sleek black shoulder.

The trainer looked at Melanie speculatively. "Since you spend so much time around here these days, maybe I ought to talk to Mr. Townsend about having you exercise a few horses for me," he said suddenly. "No reason you have to waste your time riding for every two-bit trainer in the East when you could ride for a real establishment."

Melanie was horrified at his offer. However, she kept her face carefully composed so that he had no idea how much the idea repulsed her. "Sounds interesting. We'll talk about it sometime" was all she said. Clucking slightly, she urged Image past Ralph and exhaled only when she was a safe distance away.

"Oh, Image," she murmured to her filly. "Imagine me riding for Brad! I don't think I could stand it!"

She felt guilty thinking about it, though. Even though Jazz had struck a deal regarding payment for Image's care, Melanie still never lost sight of the fact that Brad had helped her out in her time of need. As long as she spent time on the farm, she owed Townsend Acres whether she liked it or not.

I've got to make arrangements to move Image over to Whitebrook—and quickly, Melanie thought. She toyed with the end of the filly's lead rope and pushed back her sweaty hair. Then she sighed. It was hard to make plans when her time was split between the two farms. The last few days had been incredibly busy. She'd done Image's therapy, tried to groom Jinx, lunged him, and worked him in the round pen. Though Jinx was trained to do all these things, they all took twice as long as they should have, because he acted up every step of the way. Melanie wasn't about to give up, though. She wanted Ashleigh to see that he was ready to start working on the track.

Just as Melanie brought Image back to her stall, she saw Marcos, one of Townsend Acres' grooms, trotting toward her.

"You've got an urgent phone call from Whitebrook, *señorita*," he called. "Something about Jinx."

"Now what?" Melanie muttered as she handed Image's lead to the groom. "Thanks, Marcos," she called over her shoulder. She broke into a run and made her way to the nearest barn phone.

Please don't be hurt, Jinx, she prayed, grabbing the receiver. *And please don't have hurt anyone else, either.*

It was Mike. "Sorry to interrupt, but I wasn't sure when you'd be over here today. I wanted you to know that we moved Jinx out of the training barn. He kicked out his waterer and flooded several stalls."

"I'm sorry, Uncle Mike," Melanie said automatically, slumping against the barn wall. It was amazing how easy it was to apologize these days. It seemed she said she was sorry every other minute. "I'll be right over to help clean up."

Jinx will settle down, she told herself fiercely as she replaced the receiver.

"Could I ask you a huge favor? Can you put away Image for me this morning?" she asked Marcos when she returned to the filly's stall. "I've gotta go take care of something."

Marcos's dark eyes sparkled as he rubbed Image's nose. "That Jinx of yours again?"

Melanie nodded, wondering just how much the groom knew. Probably everything. The racing world's grapevine was always at work. Everyone seemed to know everyone else's business.

"I knew a horse like him in Mexico," Marcos added, massaging the filly's neck. "He was a chestnut, too. We called him El Diablo Rojo. He killed a groom. Stomped him to death."

Melanie's hand flew to her mouth. "That's horrible," she exclaimed.

Marcos nodded. "He could run like the wind, though," he said.

"Well, Jinx can run like the wind, and he's not going to kill anyone," Melanie said firmly.

With that, she made her way to her Blazer and soon was on the road to Whitebrook, driving slightly under the speed limit. She knew she ought to get there to help clean up, but she was in no hurry to face her aunt and uncle.

When Melanie entered the training barn a few minutes later, she saw Dani and Joe sweeping up piles of soaked bedding. Mike was busy with a wrench.

Melanie ducked her head, then rushed over to grab a wide broom. "Sorry again," she muttered.

No one said a word, but Melanie felt the full weight of their annoyance at her willful colt.

"Sweetie, you've just got to cut it out," Melanie told Jinx a few minutes later as she stood in front of his new stall. It was at the end of the recent addition to the stallion barn. Mike had explained that he thought it might be a better place for the restless colt. The stallion barn was built with extra reinforcements. And since there were several stalls between him and the next horse, it would be harder for Jinx to disturb the other horses.

Melanie took him out of his stall and was pleased that this time the colt stood quietly for her while she groomed him. In fact, he only lashed out at her once, when she tried again to brush his mane.

I can't figure out why he's so touchy about his mane, she thought briefly. *Maybe he's just more sensitive than most horses.*

But in her heart Melanie couldn't help thinking that maybe Jinx just didn't care what anyone else wanted. He wanted things his way, and he wasn't going to give an inch.

"There you are, Melanie."

Melanie looked up at the sound of Ashleigh's voice. Ashleigh approached the crossties but didn't come close to Jinx.

Jinx flattened his ears and lifted his front leg to strike at Ashleigh. Instead he knocked Melanie sideways and sent her flying against the wall by the crossties.

"You okay?" Ashleigh exclaimed as Melanie righted herself.

"No biggie," Melanie said quickly. She tried not to let it show how narrowly she'd missed being hurt.

Ashleigh pursed her lips. "Melanie," she began softly.

Melanie held up her hand. "It was just him trying to—"

"No," her aunt said sternly, cutting her off. "You need to look this situation squarely in the eye. This horse really could hurt you, maybe even kill you."

"But he won't," Melanie insisted. "He's just high-spirited, that's all. Plus he's been bounced from home to home, and his training hasn't been that consistent. I'm going to turn him around. You'll see."

"I just don't know," Ashleigh replied. "I've been around a lot of horses, but I've rarely seen anything like this. I'm not sure this one's redeemable."

"He is," Melanie fired back. "I just need a little time."

Ashleigh didn't appear to be convinced. "Well, we'll see," was all she said.

Melanie was relieved when her aunt and uncle left the following morning for a summer sale. They would be gone till Friday night. Though it wasn't much time, Melanie planned on using it to practice saddling Jinx and mounting him. She knew that based on the big colt's behavior so far, he probably would put up a real fight. She was determined to try to smooth things out before Ashleigh returned. Melanie was sure that if she could get him saddled and show Ashleigh that she could stay aboard, her aunt would relent. Then she'd let Melanie take the chestnut on the track.

She'll see how fast he is and realize I really can make a racehorse out of him, Melanie thought fiercely.

As soon as she arrived back at Whitebrook after walking Image, she took Jinx out of his stall and groomed him. He pinned back his ears a few times, but for once Melanie managed to untangle his mane a little before he put up real resistance.

So far so good, she thought, standing back and smiling. Over the last few days she'd made a little headway with his unkempt coat. Now for the first time she could really see his rich, deep-red hue.

"If you keep letting me work on you, you're going to be so magnificent that no one will be able to take their eyes off you," she told her colt.

Melanie started down the aisle carrying a light exercise saddle and bridle just as Dani and Joe came out of the barn office.

"What's that for?" Dani asked, glancing at the tack.

"I'm going to saddle Jinx," Melanie said calmly, daring either of them to do anything about it.

"Whoa. This I gotta see," said Joe.

He and Dani turned to follow Melanie down the aisle. Melanie scowled as she walked. She definitely didn't want an audience, though she knew neither Dani nor Joe would go running to Ashleigh. Still, she thought, it probably wouldn't hurt to have them around just in case.

"I'm going to saddle him in a stall," Melanie said. "That way, if he objects to being saddled, he'll be contained."

"Good idea," Joe replied.

As Melanie led him over to the nearest stall, Johnnie and Naomi drifted over to watch.

What is this? Melanie thought with annoyance. *A circus? Is everyone on the farm going to come for a look at the famous fierce horse?*

Trying to ignore her audience, Melanie stepped into the stall with Jinx. Dani slipped in beside her. She closed the stall door gently and reached out for the saddle and the saddle pad. Melanie toyed with the idea of asking Dani to leave but finally handed her the saddle. It would be easier if she had both hands free when she tried to bridle Jinx.

Melanie took a deep breath and turned to face the colt. He seemed to sense something was up. His nostrils worked in and out, and he grew tense when she approached.

"They say Man o' War had real saddling issues," Melanie heard Joe whisper to Naomi.

"I'll bet this guy won't be any different," replied Naomi.

Melanie tried to brush off their comments. Reaching into her pocket, she took out a carrot. He looked suspicious, but he accepted it and didn't lunge at her. She took that as a good sign. While Jinx munched, Melanie slowly ran her hands over his shoulders and neck. All the while she moved closer to his ears, knowing that this was the tricky part. Most colts didn't like anyone getting near their ears. But to her surprise Jinx stood still. Encouraged, Melanie held up the bridle. Gently she slipped the bit in his mouth and the headstall over his head.

"There," she said, standing back. "Done."

Though Jinx glared and tossed his head a little, he didn't object in a big way, as Melanie had expected.

"Wow," whispered Dani. "Who'd have thought he'd take to that so easily?"

Whew, Melanie thought. *Maybe he won't be so hard to saddle after all.*

Fifteen minutes later Melanie realized she'd been sadly mistaken. Each time she approached Jinx with the saddle, he reared and backed away. But she continued talking softly with him, stroking him when she could. Finally he allowed her to place the tiny saddle on his back. He bunched up when she tightened the girth, but he didn't put up more than token resistance.

Relieved, Melanie blew out a breath and turned to face her audience.

"Guess there wasn't much to see after all," Melanie told them. "Want your money back?"

"Are you going to get on his back?" Joe asked.

"Tomorrow," Melanie said decisively. "I want to quit on a good note."

"All right, Jinx, this is it," Melanie said to her colt the next morning. "No funny stuff."

Whitebrook's morning workouts were over, and she hoped that the staff would be busy enough so that no one would come around for part two of the circus show. She was able to saddle and bridle Jinx, but after leading the colt out to a paddock, Melanie saw Dani and Joe. They leaned against the rail, waiting expectantly for fireworks, just as they'd done the day before.

"I'll stand by in case you need help," Dani said.

Melanie wanted to be irritated, but when it came right down to it, she was glad for the offer. The last thing she wanted was to be injured. That would only set back her plans for working with the colt. What's more, it would give everybody one more reason to be down on Jinx.

Dani held the prancing colt's head, and gingerly Melanie placed her knee in the groom's hand. She felt Jinx's weight shift as she made contact with the saddle. Once aboard, she realized that she'd been holding her breath.

"Let him go," she called.

Dani released his head, and immediately the colt shot like forward like a bullet. Grimly Melanie hung on as the colt raced around the small enclosure. Sitting deeply, she closed her hands on the reins, trying desperately to control him. Jinx narrowly missed running over Dani, who scampered out of the paddock to safety.

"Easy, boy," Melanie called out to the colt while she battled to control him.

For a few seconds Jinx fought her with all the fury he could muster. Then he seemed to give, his body relaxing. Melanie brought his head up as he slowed.

After several turns around the enclosure, Melanie couldn't resist shooting a grin to Joe and Dani. Big mistake. The next second Melanie felt herself being pitched from Jinx's back as he exploded in a mighty corkscrew buck.

Melanie landed on the ground with a thump just as Jinx folded his legs and cleared the rail, whinnying shrilly. Then he tore off down the hill, bucking and twisting furiously.

"You okay?" Dani called.

Melanie sat up dazedly and nodded.

"That fool horse is heading toward the oval," yelled Joe before setting off in hot pursuit, calling out, "Loose horse!"

"Good thing there's nobody on it right now," Dani mumbled. She walked over to Melanie and helped her up.

As soon as Melanie caught her breath, she and Dani ran over to the oval. They arrived in time to see Jinx tearing down the backstretch. The stirrups banged around wildly on his sides, driving him on faster and faster. Joe stopped by the gap, waiting for the opportunity to try to catch the colt.

"Check it out. That colt of yours sure likes to run," he said quietly.

Mesmerized, Melanie nodded and sucked in her breath as the big colt swept past them. His great hooves drummed the ground like thunder. She couldn't believe what she was seeing. It was just like when she'd first met Image, two years before. The filly had broken away from her groom and shot riderless onto the track at Turfway Park. Now the same scene was replaying before her eye. This time instead of a flash of black, there was a flash of red.

A noise that sounded like a sob rose in her throat.

"Don't be too upset," Dani said, misreading Melanie's reaction and patting her shoulder.

"Upset?" Melanie gasped, shaking her head vigorously. "You don't understand. This is great!"

She knew Dani probably thought she was crazy. But for the first time since bringing Jinx home, Melanie felt heartened. After all, Image had done the same thing. She'd shaken off her restraints and shown the world what she could do—if she was left to do it on *her* terms. *And look how well that turned out!* Melanie thought with satisfaction.

No, Melanie decided once she'd finally caught her

runaway colt, this meant only one thing: Jinx might need to do things his way, but he was going to make a fine racehorse one day. She was sure of it.

Late that afternoon Melanie pounced on the phone when it rang in her cottage at Townsend Acres.

"Jazz, I'm so glad you called," she said, hearing his voice. Though she was dying to launch in immediately about Jinx and her exciting discovery, she asked about the tour instead.

"Amsterdam's a total blast!" Jazz exclaimed. Excitedly he recounted details of his last two concerts.

"Where are you off to next?" Melanie asked, trying to be polite. She knew that Pegasus was incredibly important to Jazz. Lately she'd dominated their conversations with Jinx and her own concerns.

"Belgium," Jazz replied. "More about that later. Now tell me, how's it going with our next Derby winner?"

"Great," she crowed. "He threw me today, and he tore off toward the track all by himself."

"That's not great!" Jazz cut in.

"No, you don't understand," Melanie went on. "He ran so fast. I didn't have a watch to clock him or anything, but I could tell he made amazing time. He flashed by those quarter poles like lightning."

"That's nice, Mel," Jazz said quietly. "But doesn't a horse who tosses his rider in a race get disqualified?"

"Yeah, but that's not the point," Melanie said. "The point is, he really does have speed, and he really wants to run."

She paused, expecting to hear Jazz tell her how thrilled he was. Instead what he said shocked her: "You know, Melanie, maybe we rushed into this a little too quickly."

Melanie sat up straight. "What are you talking about? This just goes to show that we *didn't* make a mistake. We've really got something here."

"Maybe," Jazz said quietly.

But Melanie could tell that he was anything but convinced. She spent the rest of the conversation trying to make him understand that he was wrong.

After hanging up the phone, Melanie curled up in a chair, flipping through the latest issue of *Bloodhorse*. Seeing an ad for the Belmont Park meet, she remembered that it ended this weekend.

I never got back there to ride, she thought uncomfortably. *And I told Christina I'd be back in a few days. Some jockey I'll make if I never have time at the track.*

Melanie chewed on her lip as she considered her next move. *I'll have to leave Jinx if I want to ride at Saratoga.*

9

SATURDAY MORNING JOE LEFT FOR BELMONT TO HAUL THE horses. This left Whitebrook short of exercise riders, so Melanie offered to help. She knew she needed to try to make up for all the trouble Jinx had caused at the farm over the last few days. And anyway, she hadn't ridden in several days. She was in danger of getting out of shape, and she needed to be ready for Saratoga. What's more, she needed to be ready to ride Jinx that day.

I'm going to ask Ashleigh right after workouts, she decided.

Melanie rode three horses. Then she took Rascal out for his morning gallop. As she piloted the four-year-old on the inside rail, she found herself eager to be finished with the workout. She wanted to corner her aunt and convince her to let her take Jinx out on the track.

I hope she doesn't give me a hard time, Melanie thought, slowing Rascal after his gallop. She handed Rascal's reins to Dani and rushed over to talk to her aunt.

To Melanie's surprise, Ashleigh nodded. "Let's see what this guy can do," she said.

"You're on!" Melanie exclaimed, darting away to get Jinx before her aunt could change her mind.

"Here's your big chance. Don't spoil things," Melanie told her colt as she groomed him. Luckily, Jinx didn't protest being saddled. He allowed himself to be led over to the gap without incident.

He'll be just fine, Melanie told herself optimistically, adjusting her helmet.

Dani appeared in the aisle just then and watched Melanie tighten her girth.

"Do you need a leg up?" asked Dani as she followed Melanie down the path to the track opening. Dani, Melanie noticed, looked as though she'd rather have root canal surgery than get close to Jinx.

"Sure," Melanie said, praying that Jinx wouldn't take a swipe at Dani.

"If he comes at me, I warn you, I'm going to have to get out of the way," Dani said, starting to cup her hand. "I know that broken bones sometimes come with the territory, but I draw the line at pulverized bones."

"But he's not *always* bad," Melanie exclaimed.

"And just when *is* he good?" Dani shot back.

"When he sleeps," Melanie replied sheepishly.

"Which is never," Dani retorted. "You know, maybe he needs a mascot."

Melanie smiled. Of course. How could she have forgotten that? Pairing a restless racehorse with an animal mascot was a time-honored practice around training barns. Image had once had a donkey named Pedro, and then later Jazz bought her a fuzzy pony named Baby. Baby had made all the difference with Image.

"Thanks for reminding me, Dani," she said, bending her leg and preparing to mount.

She grinned when she threw her leg over the saddle and Jinx stood perfectly still. And she couldn't resist throwing Dani a see-I-told-you-so look.

"A miracle!" Dani pronounced, snapping on a lead rope and leading Jinx to the gap. "But the bigger miracle will be if he lets you stay aboard once he gets out there."

"Oh, he will," Melanie said, trying to sound confident. Inside, however, her stomach was rumbling, and she felt herself tense as Jinx began bunching up, humping his back.

"Oh, no, you don't," Melanie told him, pulling his head up with the reins.

As Melanie rode Jinx out onto the track, she saw that Ashleigh was standing at the rail and Kevin was mounted on one of Whitebrook's old workhorses. Melanie realized that her aunt had taken the extra precaution because she figured Jinx was sure to cause trouble.

Everyone always expects the worst, Melanie thought irritably.

"I want you to take it easy with Jinx," Ashleigh was saying, walking along the rail toward her. "This is his first time on this track, and I don't want you to take any chances. Start out slowly and keep him from opening up too much. Just a little jog is all we want today, to let him limber up his legs a little. A controlled canter, maybe, if you feel ready."

"Sure, Aunt Ashleigh," Melanie said, licking her dry lips. She wanted to be excited that she was really riding Jinx for the first time. Instead her nerves were so tightly strung, she felt as though she was going to snap any minute.

Making her way down onto the track, Melanie was pleased when Jinx began moving out freely. He looked around, but he didn't hump his back or haul on the reins. He didn't show any signs that he was going to misbehave. In fact, if anything, he seemed to be a little lazy. Melanie nudged him with her heels, urging him forward. The sun was high, and Melanie perspired under her protective vest.

I'm not nervous, she told herself firmly. *I'm the Ice Princess, remember?*

After a morning of workouts, the track was pretty churned up. Melanie made her way carefully around the track, taking care to avoid any holes or deep areas. She wanted everything to go as well as possible.

Clucking, Melanie urged Jinx into a jog, alert in case he tried anything. After a while she glanced at her aunt. When Ashleigh nodded, Melanie urged Jinx into a canter.

Tilting forward in the saddle, Melanie balanced her weight in her stirrups, feeling Jinx's rhythmic stride. The pair cantered slowly around the bend. Suddenly Melanie felt the impulse to let him open up a little.

Sorry, Aunt Ashleigh, she thought, clucking at the big colt to make him go forward. *I just want you to see what Jinx here can do. Maybe then you'll see why I had to take a chance on him.*

But in spite of Melanie's urging, Jinx refused to move out at anything faster than a rocking-horse pace. No matter how much Melanie tried, the colt meandered around the track as if Melanie weren't cueing him at all.

Well, it's his first real day out here, Melanie thought

when Ashleigh signaled for her to bring Jinx in.

Melanie decided she'd just be grateful he hadn't thrown her or done his famous bucking act. At least this way, she'd get another chance to show everyone that they didn't need to prepare for the worst every time Jinx set foot on a track.

"Let's see how he is out of the starting gate," Ashleigh said two days later.

Melanie mounted Jinx after the morning workouts were finished. In the distance, she could see that Joe, who'd just come back from hauling horses, had wheeled the starting gate onto the track.

Approaching the gate, Melanie sat deeply in her saddle in case Jinx decided to pull any stunts. Apart from flattening his ears when Joe took his reins to load him, the colt behaved himself. He loaded calmly into the chute.

"Are you ready, big guy?" Melanie asked, pushing down her goggles. "Let's pretend we're at Keeneland, and you're about to leave the pack in the dust."

The second the gate snapped open, Melanie prepared to be propelled forward. When the colt made no move, she fell forward and down onto Jinx's shoulder. Surprised, she blinked.

"Go!" she shouted.

All Jinx did was stand there. Melanie squeezed his sides, but Jinx merely tossed his head.

"Some racehorse," Joe called out. "You sure he was gate-trained?'

"Yes!" Melanie said, feeling her cheeks heat up. "Try it again."

She maneuvered the colt out of the gate, and Joe led him back in. When the gate flew open, Jinx broke, but without any real impulsion.

"Again!" Ashleigh called out from the rail.

Joe looked disapproving as he led Jinx back once again into the chute. It didn't help matters any when Jinx swung his head and butted Joe. The blow pushed Joe forward and he almost stumbled.

"This horse never misses a chance to try to shred me, does he?" the groom grumbled, scowling.

"Sorry," Melanie said quickly.

"Let's hope he figures it out this time," Joe said, closing him into the chute.

This time when the gate snapped open, Jinx shot forward, but he immediately exploded in a series of leaps and bucks, and Melanie had to pull him in a tight circle to get him to stop.

Still, she thought, dabbing at the sweat trickling down her temples, it was clear he knew what he was supposed to do after the starting gate was opened.

Well, sort of, she added unhappily. After she galloped Jinx lightly around the track, she pulled up and walked him toward the gap.

"See? That wasn't so bad, was it?" Melanie called out to Joe.

Inside, however, she was worried. Though Jinx might spring out of the gate some of the time, what if he simply stood still the rest of the time?

"I've got to figure out what makes this horse tick!" she muttered to herself, riding toward Ashleigh.

"Seems he has some starting-gate issues," Ashleigh said.

"He's young. We'll work them out," Melanie replied, gritting her teeth.

Just then Jinx leaped sideways under her, tossing Melanie neatly to the ground. He turned back and tore down the track, the reins flapping and the stirrups banging against his sides.

"This is getting to be a bad habit with you, Jinx," Melanie exclaimed, standing up. She dusted herself off and ran toward the rail to get out of the way. Jinx lapped the track once before he decided he'd had enough.

Waiting till Jinx slowed, Melanie started toward him, waving her hands. She hoped he didn't decide to try to run her over. She called out his name, and he came to a full stop in front of her, his sides heaving.

"That was an interesting display," Ashleigh said.

"But at least no one got hurt. Let's call it a day, shall we?" With that, she turned to walk up the gravel path leading away from the oval.

"Don't say a word," Melanie muttered to Dani, who came over to take the reins from Melanie. "I'll put him away."

"He's just not happening, Mel," Ashleigh said to Melanie. She was standing by the training oval, leaning against the white rail and frowning.

It was Tuesday morning. Melanie had tried to break Jinx from the starting gate for the third time. Once again the colt had simply stood there, refusing to move until Melanie insisted. Then he'd gone forward without really engaging.

Melanie sighed and sat in her saddle, trying to keep Jinx from skittering. "I didn't expect him to be perfect overnight," she said defensively to a frowning Ashleigh.

Ashleigh rested her arms on the rail. "Nor did I," she said quietly. "But face it. This colt is a two-year-old. He's been trained, but he just refuses to do what he's told. He's got a nasty temper, and he won't even break with any consistency. He's way behind colts of his age. He's a whole lot of work, and you still don't know if you've really got anything here."

"You're wrong," Melanie said flatly, riding away from her aunt. "He's got breeding and brains and speed and everything."

"Everything, perhaps, but the willingness to run," Ashleigh said.

"How can you say that? He loves to run." Melanie countered.

"What he loves is to throw his energy into taking on the world," Ashleigh said quietly. "If he has anything left over, then he's willing to run. But that just isn't enough, Melanie."

That evening Melanie took a long soak in the bath at Townsend Acres and thought about Ashleigh's words.

She knows a lot about horses, Melanie thought angrily. *But that doesn't mean she's right all the time.*

She drained the bath and had just put on her bathrobe when the phone rang. Quickly she answered it, hoping it wasn't someone calling from Whitebrook to tell her Jinx was causing problems again.

Smiling when she heard Jazz's voice, she sat on the sofa, ready for a long, comfy chat.

"I miss you, Jazz," she said.

"I miss you, too, Melanie," Jazz replied.

He told her about the latest with his tour, and she filled him in on Image's progress.

"And Jinx?" he asked.

Melanie hesitated. "Well, he's not doing badly," she replied. "Though he doesn't seem to like the starting gate much."

"Kicked it out, huh?"

"No, not that. But he doesn't always break the way he should."

"Not good," Jazz said.

"Uh, no," Melanie admitted. "But once in a while he gets it. Then things are fine."

"Once in a while?" Jazz repeated. "I don't know, Graham. I've said it before, but I just can't help feeling that maybe we rushed into this a little too quickly."

"No way," Melanie snapped. It seemed to her that every time she talked to Jazz lately, he was trying to convince her she'd made a mistake. She was getting pretty sick of it.

"Maybe you're not being realistic enough," he said.

"Maybe you're not being supportive enough," she shot back.

After she'd hung up, she glared at the wallpaper for a long time. First it was Joe making cracks, then Dani and Ashleigh, and now Jazz. What was their problem, anyway?

Problem horses I can handle. Problem people are another matter altogether! Melanie thought huffily.

10

"IT WOULD REALLY HELP IF THIS BIG FELLOW WOULD TRY TO get some sleep," said George Ballard, Whitebrook's longtime stallion manager. "And it would be nice if he'd let the other horses get some sleep as well," he added.

It was the following day, and Melanie had just come over from Townsend Acres, where she'd worked Image in the therapy pool. She was hot and irritated. She grew even more aggravated when she saw how torn up Jinx's stall was. The big horse paced as usual, throwing bedding high up on the sides and wearing a deep groove around the stall's perimeter. It had been two weeks now since Jinx had arrived, and his barn behavior hadn't changed a bit. It was beginning to look as though he'd never settle in at Whitebrook.

"I just don't know what to do," Melanie said to the older man, pushing back her sweaty bangs. "I've been thinking about getting him a mascot, but . . . I don't know. Something keeps stopping me."

"You're worried that he might eat a mascot, right?" George Ballard's eyes pierced right through Melanie's.

"No, that's not it," Melanie said, uncomfortably aware that this was exactly the thought that had crossed her mind more than once.

"Well, then, what else could you do?"

Melanie sighed. "I can't think of anything else. I guess I'll try a mascot and see what happens. A pony like Baby could stand up to Jinx, but they're hard to find. Jazz just got lucky finding Baby."

"Well, I'd start looking," George said. "That's how you get lucky."

"There you are, Mel."

Melanie's head snapped up at the sound of Kevin's voice. He stepped into the dim interior of the barn. He was wearing his soccer clothes with his club team logo emblazoned across the front of his jersey.

"I'm heading off for a club match," he said. "I know this is kind of out of the blue and you're probably too busy, but I could use a cheering section. Want to come?"

Without thinking, Melanie nodded. She hadn't

watched a soccer game for a while. In fact, she hadn't done much of anything besides worry about horses for a while. All of a sudden, she knew she desperately needed a break. She had to clear her head. Maybe then she could think straight about everything.

"Let's go, Kevin!" she exclaimed. She marched down the barn aisle and stepped out into the sunshine, determined to forget about horses for the afternoon.

"Go, Flyerz!" Melanie cried later that afternoon.

She walked along the sidelines unable to sit as she watched the exciting match. Kevin's team was evenly matched with the other team, and the tension was high.

"That number twelve will be playing for us this season," said a man in the stands behind Melanie.

Melanie turned to look at the man and noticed his University of Kentucky sweatshirt. *That must be the university's soccer coach!* she realized.

Melanie smiled with pride as she thought about how Kevin would be leading the University of Kentucky's team to victory soon. He'd overcome a lot of obstacles—including several serious injuries and some major self-doubt—in order to get here.

He didn't give up, she said to herself as she forced herself to sit down and try to relax.

When the Flyerz made a goal, Melanie felt certain Kevin's team would maintain their lead. Now that the suspense was over, she lost interest in the game. Before she knew it, she was thinking about Jinx again.

Maybe I ought to just take the plunge and try a mascot, she thought. *If it doesn't work, at least I tried. I might not be able to find a pony right away, but maybe a goat will do in the meantime.*

Now, where to get my hands on a goat? Drumming her fingers on her jeans, Melanie suddenly remembered a farm she always passed on her way to the tack shop. With an effort, Melanie tried to remember the name. Gray's Goat Farm—that was it. Picking up her cell phone, she placed a call.

"The number for Gray's Goat Farm, please," she said.

A few minutes later the game was over, and Melanie made her way over to Kevin.

"Great game, Kevin. You were awesome," she said when she finally broke through the crowd of admiring fans.

Kevin grinned broadly. "Thanks! Hey, want to go for a soda after I shower?"

Melanie shook her head. "Sorry," she said. "I can't. I have a hot date with a nanny goat."

An elderly woman wearing a flowery straw hat who was standing nearby raised her eyebrows at Melanie's comment. Kevin doubled over with laughter.

"I have some really strange friends," he said in mock seriousness to the woman, who continued to look at Melanie disapprovingly.

Melanie frowned. "It's a pet for my horse. A mascot."

The woman sniffed and moved away quickly from Melanie.

Kevin looped his arm through hers. "That's all right," he joked. "I understand even if nobody else does."

"I just called up a place called Gray's Goat Farm," she explained, walking with Kevin toward the showers. "The lady who answered wasn't too sure about selling to me when I told her why I needed to buy a goat. I'm a little worried myself. Jinx can be kind of . . ."

"Carnivorous?" Kevin supplied.

Melanie punched him lightly but nodded. "But I promised I'd make sure the goat wouldn't be hurt."

"I'll come with you," Kevin said. "I haven't taken a girl out to a goat farm in quite a while."

Melanie laughed. "Lindsay will be jealous," she teased.

"No more than Jazz," Kevin countered before disappearing into the locker room.

When he came out, dressed in street clothes and his hair slicked back, Melanie was surprised at how handsome he looked.

Don't go there, Melanie scolded herself. *You have a boyfriend, remember? You and Kevin were over long ago.*

Just before evening feeds, Kevin and Melanie pulled down Whitebrook's driveway with Coco the nanny goat bleating in the back of the Blazer. Gray's Goat Farm, it turned out, didn't have a goat sturdy enough for what Melanie had in mind. Luckily, Kevin had remembered seeing an ad for another goat farm. When Melanie set eyes on Coco at Cooper's Goats, she knew she'd found just what she was looking for.

When they put the brown goat in the paddock where Jinx had been turned out, Melanie held her breath. She got ready to spring into the enclosure to save the goat if necessary. Coco pulled at tufts of grass while Jinx regarded her out of the corner of his eye. Walking over to her, he sniffed her, but immediately turned away.

"That's that," Melanie muttered.

"Not so fast," Kevin replied.

Jinx swung his hindquarters around and walked to the other end of the paddock.

"He isn't interested," Melanie declared after a while.

Kevin shrugged. "Let's not rush it. It just might take some more time."

128

Though Melanie and Kevin stuck around to watch the pair, Jinx continued to ignore Coco. When she ambled over to snatch at a tuft of grass near his feet, he pinned his ears and walked over to the opposite end of the paddock. Then he filled the night air with several plaintive whinnies.

"He's telling us he's still lonely. He doesn't care about Coco at all," Melanie said, her shoulders slumping. "Well, at least he didn't eat her."

Kevin nodded. "Guess she'll have to find employment somewhere else."

"Looks like I'll have to figure out what's next," Melanie replied. "Know any mule farms? Or got any ideas where I could find a pony like Baby—cheap?"

"That, Graham, could be a little harder for me to find, and the finder's fee will be higher," Kevin joked, putting a rope around the goat's neck. "You still owe me a soda for finding you a goat buff enough to stand up to Jinx."

"Forget you, Kevin," Melanie protested. "Jinx didn't like Coco, so I don't owe you a thing!"

"Yes, you do," Kevin insisted, leading the goat away. "It was for *finding* a goat. I didn't say she had to work out. That wasn't part of the deal."

Melanie was too discouraged to reply, but Kevin still managed to make her smile.

Two days later Kevin found a pony. The owner, the sister of a guy on Kevin's soccer team, was willing to lend him out on a trial basis. The pony, a brown-and-white retired child's hunter, was turned out with a number of other horses and got along with all of them.

"Meet Chipper," Kevin exclaimed to Melanie as he pulled the rig into Whitebrook's stable area. Jumping out of the cab, he dropped the ramp and unloaded the pony.

He's absolutely perfect, Melanie thought, studying Chipper's good-natured expression.

Though Jinx had shown no interest in the goat, the minute Chipper was placed in the paddock with him, he immediately walked over. Then he sniffed the little creature intently.

Come on, let this be the one, Melanie prayed.

Her heart plummeted to her paddock boots as Jinx suddenly flattened his ears and nipped the pony in the shoulder. Chipper wasn't hurt, but he squealed indignantly. Melanie and Kevin stood poised by the gate, ready to intervene if anything else happened. For a few moments Jinx merely eyed the little gelding with a malevolent glare. Then he snaked out his head and opened his jaws, this time going for a more determined attack. The pony whirled around and kicked, nicking Jinx's chest area with a tiny hoof. Neighing shrilly, he wheeled away. Enraged, Jinx immediately charged after him.

"Oh, no! He's going to hurt that little guy," Melanie burst out. She leaped to her feet and waved her arms frantically to stop Jinx.

Jinx screeched to a halt, sending up a cloud of dust. Kevin quickly removed the pony.

"Back he goes," he said, leading Chipper away. "Man, Graham. I don't know what to tell you."

Scowling, Melanie turned back to Jinx. "You are a big meanie," she scolded the horse. Jinx arched his neck and pawed the ground. It was clear he was proud that he'd scared off the pony.

Kevin loaded Chipper back in the trailer, and Melanie watched sadly as he drove off.

I guess I can't do things with Jinx the way I did with Image after all, she thought. *They are totally different, just like everyone says.*

After finishing her barn chores at Whitebrook, Melanie drove toward Townsend Acres. It was late and she was tired. Jinx and the mascot failures had pretty much zapped her strength. The lights of the oncoming cars seemed particularly bright, and she squinted as she drove. She stopped behind a car at a stoplight.

Suddenly, to her horror, she saw the driver of that

car open the car door. He shoved a tan-colored dog onto the side of the road. The instant the light changed, the driver sped off, the red taillights of the car disappearing into the night.

I can't believe I just saw that! Melanie thought, her eyes widening. *What kind of a person would dump a dog right on one of the busiest roads in Lexington?*

Melanie swerved to avoid the terrified animal, who ran onto the road, dodging the oncoming cars.

"That poor little thing is going to get hit!" gasped Melanie.

Tears springing to her eyes, she pulled over as soon as she could. Jumping out of the car, she left the door open and scanned the road frantically. Several trucks roared past, blowing her back.

"Slow down!" Melanie called out futilely, but her words were whipped away in the wake of the huge trucks.

When the dog bolted across the street toward her, Melanie whistled softly to him.

"Please come here," she pleaded.

The little dog paid no attention and ran past her. Melanie crouched down and continued trying to cajole the dog over. He turned abruptly and dashed across the road again. Then he stopped in the middle of the road, his eyes reflecting in the bright headlights. Several cars swerved around him.

Please don't get hit! Melanie prayed, expecting to hear a sickening thud any second.

She waited till there was a break in the traffic and then shot across the street. When she approached, the dog leaped away from her. He crossed to the other side of the road again. How he made it through the lanes of traffic without being struck by a car, Melanie didn't know. She had to stand at the side of the road for several minutes before the road was clear again. Finally she darted back across the road to the Blazer. For a few minutes she stood on the shoulder peering into the night. There was no sign of the dog anywhere. A sob rose to her throat.

Had the poor creature been hit by a truck and dragged down the road? The thought was so horrible, Melanie could hardly breathe.

Defeated, Melanie crawled into her car and slumped against the steering wheel. The next second she felt a wet nose on her neck, and she nearly screamed with fright. Looking over, she saw the dog sitting in the passenger seat. His tongue lolled and his sides heaved.

Quickly Melanie slammed her door, which made the dog cringe and scoot away from her.

"I'm sorry, sweetheart," Melanie crooned, reaching her hand out.

For the next half hour Melanie sat patting the dog.

She ran her hand rhythmically over his rough coat, talking in a low voice. At first the little animal shook, but gradually he calmed down, and even thrust his nose under Melanie's hand. Peering closer, Melanie tried to guess what breed the dog might be, but she couldn't tell.

"You're kind of an all-American mutt, I guess. You poor skinny thing," Melanie murmured, feeling his ribs and examining a hairless area around his neck. It was clear that the dog had had something tied too tightly around his neck—a collar, perhaps, or maybe a rope.

"Someone abused you," Melanie whispered, a great sadness welling up inside her.

Not sure what to do next, Melanie started up the Blazer and continued down the road to Townsend Acres. Suddenly she paused and pulled into the parking lot of a convenience store.

"I can't take you to Townsend Acres," she said aloud. "Brad and Lavinia would have a fit if I brought something without a pedigree a mile long onto their property." She paused, considering her options.

"I know where I'll take you! I just hope Aunt Ashleigh doesn't mind a new addition to the farm."

With that, Melanie turned around, driving back the way she came. As she drove, she talked softly to soothe the dog, who crept closer to her on the seat. He panted as he looked around anxiously. It seemed to Melanie that he was wondering what horrible thing was going to happen next.

When Melanie drove down Whitebrook's long driveway, she saw the lights on in her aunt's house. The barn was bathed in soft vapor lights, lending an eerie greenish cast to the place. Pulling up next to the stallion barn, Melanie cut the engine.

When Melanie opened the car door, the dog leaped out. Immediately he sat in the dirt next to the Blazer, awaiting Melanie's next move.

Melanie hesitated as she glanced at the house. Her aunt and uncle were kindhearted people, but Melanie knew she had tested their patience lately. What would they say when she asked if they would mind adopting an abandoned dog?

Here goes nothing, Melanie thought, squaring her shoulders. Just as she started toward the house, she heard a banging noise. It was coming from the stallion barn.

Oh, Jinx, now what are you up to? Melanie thought, feeling the familiar sensation of dread in her stomach. She changed direction and started instead toward the sound. "Come on, doggie. Let's go see what my nutzoid horse is doing before he tears down another barn."

The dog's nose went to the ground and he sniffed intently as he followed Melanie into the barn. Melanie frowned as she heard Jinx rattling around in his stall. Clearly he was stirring up the other horses as well. Several stallions were pacing their stalls, snorting and pawing the ground. Terminator, Whitebrook's most aggressive stallion, was really putting up a fuss.

Oh, great, Melanie thought. *Jinx and Terminator are having a duel to see who's the biggest bad act in the barn.* Any day now George would put his foot down and kick Jinx out of the stallion barn.

Fine, Melanie thought irritably. *If that happens, Jinx can just go into a paddock full time. He'll be happier there, anyway, just like Image is happiest in a paddock.* But in Melanie's heart she knew that wasn't a good solution. If Jinx was to ever go to the track, he'd have to be in a stall.

The dog trotted behind her all the way down the barn aisle, his tail sweeping side to side. When they went past Terminator's stall, the big black horse rammed the wall. The little dog yelped in fear and surprise.

"Calm down, Terminator, you big bully," Melanie scolded the stallion.

At the sound of her voice, Jinx sounded a trumpeting, imperious neigh. Melanie was thrilled. *He recognizes me!* she thought fleetingly.

"Hey, Jinx," Melanie called out as she and the dog approached his stall.

Throwing back the latch, Melanie opened the door. Immediately the dog rushed into the stall.

"Aagh! You weren't supposed to do that!" Melanie called out, instantly alarmed. But it was too late. The dog trotted over to the far corner of the stall. Jinx swung around, facing the intruder, his ears flattening.

Jinx is going to kill the little guy! Melanie thought, fear gripping her throat like an icy hand.

But as the big colt approached the dog, the dog's tail wagged so hard, his whole body wriggled. He showered Jinx's muzzle with a series of licks, and the chestnut stepped back. Clearly he was surprised. Lowering his head once again, he thrust his muzzle at the dog. Melanie noticed that Jinx's ears flicked forward.

Melanie held her breath, trying to figure out how she could enter the stall. She wanted to whisk away the dog, but she didn't want to get stomped. Then she began to see that something was happening between Jinx and the dog.

"You two are making friends!" Melanie gasped in amazement.

She remained quiet while the two sniffed each other thoroughly. Finally the dog jumped up into the feed bin. He turned around and curled up, shoving his nose under his furry tail. Jinx ambled over and stood over the dog protectively. Melanie hardly dared to breathe. After a while she could see the big colt's eyes close and his lower lip droop.

Melanie wasn't sure how long she stood there watching Jinx and the dog. She became aware that it was getting late. Her muscles were cramping from standing so long.

"I guess you guys don't need me," she murmured, stepping out of the stall.

She sat on a tack box and leaned against the wall, dozing on and off, ready to spring up at the slightest noise. But Jinx slept, and slowly the rest of the barn quieted down.

The next thing Melanie was aware of was the rattling of feed pans. It was followed shortly by the sound of the feed cart coming down the aisle. Opening her eyes, Melanie saw that it was morning.

I fell asleep on top of a tack box! Melanie thought. She groaned as she moved her stiff muscles.

Suddenly she was looking up into Joe's face.

"Decided your digs at Hotel Townsend Acres weren't fancy enough?" he joked.

"Too fancy, maybe," Melanie replied, looking into Jinx's stall.

The dog was now standing at the stall door, wagging his tail. Jinx was next to him, interested in his food but watching the dog to make sure he didn't go anywhere.

Joe peered into the stall. "A dog?" he said, raising his eyebrows.

Melanie ran her hand through her tousled hair and nodded. "Yeah. This is Jinx's new stablemate."

Joe opened the door and tossed in the feed. The dog shot out of the barn but returned quickly and scratched to be let back in.

"He's not the best-looking mascot I've ever seen," Joe said, opening the stall door again to admit him.

"True," Melanie said wryly. She smiled when she saw that Jinx's bedding wasn't torn up the way it had been every morning since he'd arrived at Whitebrook. "But check it out! Jinx slept all night!"

"Unbelievable!" Joe exclaimed. "But it doesn't change the fact that his mascot is still appearance-challenged."

"Don't listen to Joe, little dog," she said, stepping into the stall and scratching the shaggy creature's ears. "I think you're beautiful!"

11

"ARE YOU READY?" ASHLEIGH ASKED MELANIE AS SHE prepared to unsnap Jinx's lead rope.

Throat dry, Melanie nodded. She adjusted her goggles and gathered her reins.

It was Tuesday morning, and she was about to take Jinx out onto the Whitebrook training oval. This time Jinx was going to work with other horses. Joe was already jogging Fast Gun along the rail, and Dani was riding Rascal. Both horses had been chosen because they were Whitebrook regulars whose track behavior was consistent. Ashleigh explained that she wanted to avoid introducing any unnecessary problems till they had worked out Jinx's tendency to lash out at his opponents on the track.

"Now, don't try to do too much today," Ashleigh instructed Melanie. "Take your time with your warm-up, and I'll signal you when it's time to join the others."

Melanie fiddled with her helmet strap while she rode through the gap, feeling her hands get clammy inside her gloves. She took care to keep Jinx off by himself while she warmed him up. She knew that it was only a matter of minutes before Jinx would be next to the others, and they would both be put to the test.

"Please be good," Melanie murmured. If only she could delay the inevitable and simply breeze Jinx by himself. But she knew that if she was ever going to race the colt, she'd have to get him to race alongside competition without incident.

I've made lots of headway with him so far. Nothing here I can't handle, Melanie thought. She tried to buoy herself as Ashleigh motioned her to move closer to the other horses.

She felt Jinx bunch up beneath her as they drew closer to Fast Gun.

"Don't be afraid to be firm with Jinx," Ashleigh called out, frowning.

Melanie tightened her hands on the reins, and the colt immediately fought for his head.

"Come on, boy. I don't want to start a quarrel with you," Melanie said pleadingly.

Jinx seemed to settle at the sound of her voice, but Melanie could tell he was very aware of the gelding now pacing him. As she took the colt around the first turn, he leaped sideways, making a lunge for the gelding. This caused Melanie's foot to come out of the stirrup. She tried to slip her foot back into the stirrup, but Jinx skittered around under her, making the task impossible.

Pulling up on the outside, where she'd be out of the way, Melanie leaned over slightly to replace her foot. But just as she touched the iron, Jinx threw up his head, smacking Melanie soundly in the nose.

"Ouch!" Melanie cried, feeling tears spring to her eyes from the pain. Though her vision was blurred, she finally managed to replace her foot in the stirrup. Ashleigh gestured for her to canter and join the others.

Clucking, Melanie urged Jinx to canter, and she was relieved when the horse responded willingly. For a few seconds she felt the cool morning wind on her cheeks and reveled in the sensation of riding her beautiful, if willful, new colt.

But her reverie was cut short when Dani, riding Rascal, came along on the outside. Immediately Jinx shook his head threateningly at Rascal and pulled to the right, intent on crowding the other horse.

"Watch him!" Dani shouted, riding evasively while Melanie fought to keep Jinx from cutting over.

"Sorry!" Melanie called back. Her words flew back down her throat when Jinx broke stride and did a few crow hops.

"That horse of yours isn't a racehorse. He's road rage on hooves," Joe muttered when he drew up. He glared at Jinx out of the corner of his eye.

"We'll show you a racehorse," Melanie said, her blood surging as she joined Joe and Dani, who were forming a starting line. Though Melanie took care to keep Jinx straight, the minute he got in line next to Fast Gun he swung his hindquarters toward the other colt and poised himself to launch a kick. Acting quickly, Melanie closed her hands on the reins and dug her heel sharply into his side, causing him to move away just in time.

"Jeez, you hate everyone," Melanie muttered to the colt. "Sorry," she added, glancing at Joe. But Joe merely shook his head in disgust. Melanie couldn't blame him. No jockey liked to have his horse harassed when he was getting ready to run. When Jinx jostled Fast Gun again, Melanie felt herself grow desperate.

C'mon, Aunt Ashleigh, Melanie thought impatiently, waiting for the starting signal and watching the track between Jinx's ears. *I can't hold this half-ton time bomb much longer.*

The second her aunt's hand fell, Melanie gave Jinx rein, and the big colt leaped forward.

Now we'll give them something to stare at, Melanie thought with satisfaction. Jinx galloped down the track, pulling slightly ahead of Fast Gun and Rascal.

"Pour it on, Jinx!" Melanie cried, balancing over his shoulders and leaning lower onto his neck. When she heard the drumroll of hooves approaching from behind, Melanie felt her adrenaline kick into gear.

"We've got to go for it!" she cried, asking Jinx for more speed. But instead of surging ahead, Jinx slowed. In a split second Fast Gun caught up with him, followed by Rascal along the inside rail. Jinx responded by trying to carom off each horse. Melanie winced in pain as Jinx bumped Dani's horse.

"Handle him, Mel," Dani cried out, plainly alarmed.

"I'm trying," Melanie yelled back, struggling to straighten out the big, unruly colt before someone got hurt. It was hard to do when he was hurtling along at a full gallop. Glancing up, Melanie could see Ashleigh frantically signaling the group to slow. She knew her aunt was trying to call off the race before someone got hurt. After Fast Gun and Rascal dropped back, Melanie started to pull up Jinx. But the colt, instead of slowing, suddenly shot ahead and bolted down the track.

He's running away! Melanie thought grimly. Sitting back in her saddle, she began to apply a pulley rein, fighting to slow the colt. When she was finally able to bring him down, he darted sharply to the left. Instinctively Melanie closed her hand on the right rein, but Jinx skittered on. He began cantering sideways and forward at the same time, crabwise. Though Melanie felt herself slipping, she clenched her teeth and forced herself to stay in the saddle.

"I'm not going to let you toss me," she scolded the horse as he continued raging down the track. "You've got to listen!"

Just as Melanie felt she was regaining some control, the other horses approached and Jinx leaped sideways again. He knocked against Fast Gun, throwing him off stride. When Melanie was finally able to bring Jinx down, she glanced back in time to see Joe slow Fast Gun and swing off his back. Quickly he ran his hand down Fast Gun's leg and stopped at his fetlock area.

"Oh, no, Fast Gun's hurt!" Melanie gasped. "Jinx, what have you done?"

Jinx tossed his head defiantly. He strained to break her hold and start galloping again, but Melanie held fast. Worry welled up inside her, threatening to cut off her breath. If anything happened to Fast Gun, she thought, she wouldn't be able to stand it.

Ashleigh ran out onto the track and bent down to look closely at the gelding's fetlock. Fast Gun, Melanie could see, was putting no weight on his right leg.

"Please, please, be okay," Melanie gulped while she brought her lathered colt to a walk. She climbed off, pulled Jinx's reins over his head, and walked through the gap.

Maureen Mack, Whitebrook's assistant trainer, met her with a cooler. "What the heck happened out there?" she asked, gazing over to where Joe was leading a limping Fast Gun off the track. Dani was leading Rascal behind, her face a pale mask.

"I don't know," Melanie said in a tight voice. She took off her saddle and tossed the cooler over Jinx's back.

Maureen shook her head and shot past her. She placed coolers over Rascal and Fast Gun and asked if there was anything she could do to help.

"How bad?" Melanie asked as Joe sprinted past her to call the vet and get a first-aid kit.

"Can't tell yet," Joe replied.

Melanie bit her lip while she walked Jinx around the training barn to cool him down. Her stomach churned sickeningly. While she circled, she saw Joe return with the first-aid kit. She watched as Ashleigh applied some medication and swathed Fast Gun's fetlock with a bandage.

If he's really hurt, Aunt Ashleigh will never forgive me, Melanie thought miserably. *She's been telling me that Jinx is a mistake ever since I got him. So has everybody else, for that matter*. She looked over at Jinx, and her eyes filled with tears.

Could they be right? she wondered, feeling her heart sink into her boots. Just then she saw the vet's truck pull into the stable area.

As soon as Melanie had finished putting Jinx away, she ducked into the barn office to find out what the vet had said.

"Bone chip," her aunt told her.

"I'm so sorry," Melanie whispered. A bone chip, she knew, could be an insignificant injury requiring rest and cold packs—or it could be serious.

Ashleigh drummed her fingers on her desk. "He'll probably need surgery. And then he'll be laid up for six weeks, maybe eight," she said quietly, looking off into space.

Melanie hung her head and waited for Ashleigh to tell her to get her colt off the property right then. But Ashleigh didn't say a thing. After a few minutes Melanie left the office in a heartsick daze.

12

MELANIE KNEW THAT SHE NEEDED TO FILL JAZZ IN ON WHAT had happened that morning on the track, but she was anything but eager to place the call to his hotel in Belgium. All afternoon and into the evening she put it off. Finally she knew she couldn't delay any longer.

"Fast Gun will need arthroscopic surgery and then a huge lay-up?" Jazz asked after hearing the story. "Ashleigh must be furious."

"Well, she wasn't very happy, that's for sure," Melanie replied.

"No, I imagine she wouldn't be—Fast Gun is a Whitebrook favorite," Jazz said.

"Yeah," Melanie mumbled. After a pause, she tried to change the subject. "So, how's the tour going?"

"Fine. But right now I'm more concerned about Jinx," Jazz replied, refusing to be redirected. "That horse doesn't let up for a minute, does he?"

"This is how it was with Image," Melanie said in a rush. "Things just seemed to happen around her. But you have to admit it came out all right."

"Melanie," Jazz interrupted, "c'mon. This horse *is* a four-legged jinx. You've said yourself that Image was just high-spirited. This horse does actual damage. And what's more, it's like he gets a *charge* out of hurting his competition."

"That's not true!" Melanie retorted. "He's a little bit of a rebel—"

"He's more than a rebel, and you know it!"

"Okay, so he's more than a rebel," Melanie confessed. "But he's not the monster you're making him out to be. You haven't even seen him and already you've written him off."

"Maybe I have." Jazz spoke calmly. "Mel, I hate to say it, but I think it's time to cut our losses. Now, before he does something worse to another horse. Or pounds you to the ground. Or gets banned from the track or something."

Melanie couldn't believe what she was hearing. "What? Cut our losses? What losses? I've just gotten this colt. I've hardly had time to work with him," she sputtered.

"Yeah, and see what's happened in such a short time," Jazz came back. "No telling what will happen in the next two weeks!"

"Maybe I'll make some progress, that's what could happen," Melanie retorted. She could feel her heart pounding so loudly, she wondered if Jazz could hear it all the way in Belgium. "He's a winner, and he just needs a chance. I know I can break through if I just have more time."

"No," Jazz went on. "I think we should sell quickly and find another horse at the fall auctions. One that's the whole package: brains, speed, beauty—and temperament!"

"He *is* the whole package," Melanie insisted. "His temperament will be fine once I figure out what makes him tick."

"Melanie, you're not being reasonable," Jazz said pleadingly.

"You're the one who's not being reasonable!" she shot back.

After Melanie hung up the phone, she grabbed her pillow savagely and flung it against the wall.

The next morning Melanie was at Townsend Acres, giving Image her daily walk on the grass, when she saw Brad and Lavinia come out of the main house.

They both wore tennis whites, and Lavinia sported a gold-and-diamond tennis racquet on a glittery chain around her neck.

Lord and Lady Townsend are probably off to the country club, Melanie thought, watching them load the car with their tennis gear.

Lavinia climbed into Brad's sleek sports car. But to Melanie's dismay, Brad headed over toward the grassy area where she was hand-walking Image.

As he approached, Melanie caught a whiff of Brad's expensive cologne.

"The good doc keeps telling me how pleased he is at Image's recovery," Brad began conversationally. Melanie saw that he took care not to step onto the grass and stain his pristine shoes.

"Yes, she seems to be feeling good, and she's walking perfectly on that leg," Melanie said. "Thank you again for everything you've done for her."

Brad dismissed her words with a wave of his hand. "I hear you've got trouble on hooves that goes by the name of Jinx."

Melanie sighed. The grapevine was hard at work, as usual. No doubt the Townsends had heard every word about what Jinx had done to Fast Gun.

Melanie was just about to reply when she saw Brad whip out his checkbook.

"Let me do you another favor. How much for me to

take him off your hands?" he asked without warning.

Melanie blinked. "Excuse me?"

Brad's face looked harsh in the morning sun. "How much?" he repeated. "He's not worth much, bad actor that he is. Still, he's got Man o' War lines, and those aren't to be sniffed at. I've got people here who can knock his attitude right out of him."

Melanie fixed him with a cold stare. "I heard you tell someone you already had more winners than you could handle and that you didn't need any more," she said defiantly. "That's why you didn't buy him in the first place."

Brad shrugged. "So I changed my mind. I'm feeling a little restless now that the Triple Crown is over. I could use a new challenge. Anyway, I talked to my accountant, and he says I need to spend more money."

"Jinx is not for sale," she said calmly.

Brad sneered. "Everyone's got a price," he replied. "He's an unproven colt with a bad reputation. He could be worthless. I'm offering to take him off your hands. Consider it charity. Not many people would do that."

"He's not for sale," Melanie said with more force. She turned away, leading Image a little faster than usual, but taking care not to let her break into a trot.

"Once a fool . . . " Brad said.

Melanie waited till she heard the purr of the sports car's engine before she turned around. Then she glared daggers at the retreating car.

When she got to Whitebrook later that morning, she went straight to Jinx's paddock. She was just about to slip through the rails when she saw her aunt approach.

"How's Fast Gun doing today?" Melanie inquired.

Ashleigh shrugged. "No real change. Still some swelling. He's on some pain medication, and we're icing him down till he's taken in for surgery."

Melanie was silent. There just wasn't anything more to say. How many times could she apologize? she wondered.

"Brad just offered to buy Jinx, but I turned that down quickly," she said to Ashleigh. She figured her aunt would probably roll her eyes at how Brad was always on the lookout for a good deal.

But what Ashleigh said instead was, "I think you ought to take him up on the offer, at whatever price."

"What?" Melanie said. She knew Ashleigh was mad at Jinx, but she still couldn't believe her aunt would want her to sell him to Brad.

"Melanie," Ashleigh said, looking her straight in the eye, "Mike and I talked last night. I know you don't want to hear this, but there's no way around it.

We just can't have Jinx at Whitebrook anymore. I'm sorry, but you'll have to sell him or find him another place to stay."

"That's not fair!" Melanie exclaimed, staring at her aunt.

"What's not fair is having a horse like him on the property, terrorizing grooms and risking the other horses," Ashleigh said, a pained look on her face. "It's too much of a liability, Melanie. You have to face it. There's definitely an element of risk in the racehorse business, but Jinx is raising the stakes way beyond what we can afford."

When Melanie didn't reply, Ashleigh went on, this time in a softer tone. "Melanie, you know I rarely give up on a horse. And I know you don't give up easily, either. I saw how much you believed in Pirate and Trib and then Image. It's a good thing to pour your heart and soul into a horse and want to bring out his best in spite of difficulties. But some horses are heartbreakers, plain and simple. And if you're going to be in the business for the long haul, you've got to know when it's time to walk away."

"It's too early to walk away," Melanie protested. "I've only had Jinx for a little over a couple of weeks."

"And a long couple of weeks at that," Ashleigh said with a sigh. "I'm sorry, Melanie. I know it seems harsh, but you've got two days to get him out of here."

With that, Ashleigh turned and walked toward the training barn. Melanie stared at her aunt's back, fury building inside her. Her aunt and uncle were supposed to be on her side! How could they do this to her?

Well, I'm not going to give up without a fight, Melanie thought defiantly. If she couldn't keep Jinx at Whitebrook, she'd just move him somewhere else.

Whisperwood? she thought, considering the stable Samantha Nelson owned with her husband, Tor. No, it was an eventing farm, not set up to handle a racehorse. *Tall Oaks?* she mused, considering the farm where Ian's stepdaughter, Cindy McLean, was head trainer. No, the owner, Ben al-Rihani, would never stand for a horse like Jinx injuring his stock.

Trouble is, no one I know would have a horse like Jinx in the barn, she thought, the reality hitting her like a runaway rig.

"If Aunt Ashleigh makes you leave Whitebrook, I'll have to sell you," Melanie cried out.

Turning to Jinx, she buried her face in his coppery shoulder and started sobbing uncontrollably. The big horse swung his head toward her, and for a split second she expected him to try to bite her. Instead he nibbled her shoulder gently and inhaled deeply, letting out a sigh that made his whole body shudder.

"Oh, Jinx," she cried. "Is it possible to love a horse so much that it totally overrides your good sense?"

• • •

Melanie slept fitfully that night, and at four A.M., when she'd been lying wide awake staring at her ceiling, she finally sat up. Throwing back her covers, she stood and dressed quickly. A few minutes later she was on her way to Whitebrook.

I've got to try to change Aunt Ashleigh's mind, she thought grimly, getting out of the Blazer and making her way to Jinx's stall.

13

"I'M SO SORRY," DANI CALLED OUT AS SHE AND MELANIE jogged around the Whitebrook oval. "I heard you have to get rid of Jinx."

"I know you're not sorry," Melanie countered. "You're probably happy to see him go." She knew she was being unfair to Dani, but she couldn't help it. Just thinking of selling Jinx was more than she could handle.

Dani didn't speak for a moment. Then she said, "Well, I have to admit it gives me some relief to have him gone. It's kind of nerve-racking, always wondering when he's going to go after me or one of the other horses. But I *am* sorry for you. I know how much he means to you."

Melanie shrugged and balanced herself in her stirrups, considering Dani's words. Then she turned her focus on maintaining an even pace. When Jinx had first set foot on the oval that morning, he'd exploded in a series of bucks. Now he'd settled down somewhat, and Melanie was determined to keep him calm.

Glancing up, she could see Ashleigh and Maureen talking at the rail, giving some last-minute instructions to Joe. Joe was mounted on a two-year-old named Speedalight. She was about to turn back to Jinx when she saw Kevin walk up next to Ashleigh. He grinned at Melanie, giving her a thumbs-up. For some reason her heart flip-flopped.

Kevin's cheering for me, Melanie thought with a flash of pleasure. She was amazed at how nice it was to have his support after all the grief she was getting from everyone else—including Jazz.

"Come on, boy," she whispered to her colt. "Aunt Ashleigh is watching. Try to behave just once, and maybe she'll reconsider."

At the sound of her voice, Jinx tossed his head.

"Keep him away from us today, okay, Mel?" Dani asked, and urged on the filly she was riding.

Melanie narrowed her eyes and closed her fingers on the reins slightly. Ashleigh had already made it clear to Melanie that she wasn't to get near any of the other horses that morning.

After taking the colt for a circuit around the oval at a jog, Melanie pushed him into a canter. Immediately Jinx slowed, his ears flattening.

"Quit it," Melanie howled in frustration, glancing at her aunt. Luckily, Ashleigh seemed to be watching Speedalight instead. "Jinx, you can't do this to me!"

When Joe and Speedalight passed them, Jinx snaked his head sharply in their direction, nearly yanking the reins out of Melanie's gloved hands. "No, you don't," Melanie commanded. "They weren't even near us."

Prancing sideways, Jinx tossed his head. Melanie urged the colt forward and tried to straighten him, but he ignored her. He pulled back to evade her hand, then spurted forward. Grimly Melanie continued trying to bring him into line, using every riding technique she knew, but to no avail. He continued zigzagging down the track, speeding up and then slowing down. When Melanie tried to rein him in, he fought her, trashing around and nearly unseating her.

"It's always the same with you, isn't it?" Melanie said savagely under her breath. She could feel her frustration boiling over. "You've got to take on everyone. You've got to strike out at every horse you see. When your rider wants to go forward, you want to go backward. When someone wants you to go straight, you're determined to shoot sideways. Can't you just focus on racing? That's what you were bred to do, you know!"

Without looking over to the rail, Melanie knew her aunt was probably watching Jinx's antics and congratulating herself on making the right decision to send him on his way.

Suddenly Melanie slumped in her saddle, feeling so weary she could hardly stand it. What was she holding on for? A horse that hated everyone and would probably be banned from the track the next time anyone tried to race him? A horse that put all his energy into shredding others instead of throwing his heart into running? So what if he was starting to respond to her on the ground? The minute she got on his back, he seemed to forget that she was the one who believed in him. And he probably wouldn't ever change.

This isn't Image. This isn't another Man o' War, Melanie thought sadly. *Jinx is a throwback to Hastings, one of the most unreachable horses in history. In the end, breeding always comes through.*

"Well, that's that," she muttered, threading the reins through her hands and giving up. "I guess Aunt Ashleigh's right. Have it your way, boy. I'm tired of fighting you. Guess you don't want to stay here at Whitebrook after all."

Feeling the slack in his reins, Jinx began speeding up. As he approached Dani's filly from behind, he sud-

160

denly thrust himself forward, neatly passing the filly. This time he didn't make a move toward her. Instead he surged onward in a straight line, his huge, ground-eating strides pounding the ground faster and faster.

He's bolting again! Melanie thought as a pole flashed by. For a fleeting second she readied herself to sit back and slow Jinx. Suddenly, without making a conscious decision to do so, Melanie rose in her stirrups. Leaning forward, she let her body go with the motion. What did it matter what she did now? It was over. She'd probably find herself in the dirt in a few seconds. By this time the next day, she'd be making plans to sell Jinx. Not to Brad, that was for sure, but to someone who wanted to take a chance the way she had. And soon Jinx would be a distant memory, the only horse she'd ever had to give up on.

"We could have had some nice races together," Melanie murmured to the colt, feeling tears well up behind her mud-splattered goggles. "Look how fast you're running, boy."

As they came around the far turn, Melanie could see Joe ahead of her, galloping Speedalight along the inside rail. Jinx sped up and gained on the colt, passing him and continuing at top speed, swerving every so often.

After Jinx completed a circuit, Melanie could tell he was half expecting her to slow him, but she decided against it. There was no point. He'd probably just fight her some more, and she was beyond caring. By now her goggles were so obliterated by mud, she could hardly see. She rode by instinct, perching precariously in her saddle as Jinx dipped and made his way down the track, running as if demons were pursuing him. Would he never tire? she wondered. He'd run almost two miles!

Melanie caught a fleeting glimpse of Ashleigh, who was standing at the rail, gaping. She also caught sight of Kevin, and for a split second their eyes met in a way that left Melanie feeling vaguely uneasy. Several people had gathered around Ashleigh, but Melanie didn't have time to see who they were.

It's circus time again, and everyone's come to watch the freak show, just like before, Melanie thought briefly. She dropped the reins altogether in a gesture of total surrender.

Finally Melanie became aware that Jinx was slowing. He brought himself down to a canter, then a jog and a walk. His neck was lathered, and he blew mightily. Still, Melanie made no move to pick up the reins. Confused because he was getting no signals from his rider, Jinx came to a stop.

"You want to call all the shots? Well, then, you figure out what to do," Melanie murmured, her heart pounding in her chest. Catching her breath, she realized that for the first time ever Jinx was trying to do what his rider wanted instead of insisting upon doing what *he* wanted.

"You see, Jinx?" she said triumphantly. "It's supposed to be a partnership. You and me, pal. Not just you. Not just me."

Jinx tossed his head impatiently, but Melanie refused to cue him in any way. Finally, with his head down, the colt started forward and ambled uncertainly toward the gap.

"What happened out there?" Ashleigh called out, rushing over. Automatically she reached for Jinx's head, but Melanie shook her away.

"Wait, Aunt Ashleigh. Let him be. I want to see what he's going to do next," she said.

The next second Melanie caught sight of Jazz. His eyes were red-rimmed, and he looked exhausted. "What? You're supposed to be in Europe," she sputtered.

Quickly she darted a glance at Kevin, who was plainly uncomfortable at Jazz's presence.

Jazz shrugged. "I couldn't stand it. I caught a plane. I had to come home and see what the fuss was all about. Guess I saw it."

Melanie's thoughts were a tangle of confusion. She wanted to question Jazz some more, and she wanted say something to Kevin, though she wasn't sure what.

Instead she turned her attention back to Jinx. The big colt made his way slowly toward his stall, his sides heaving and his head drooping lower and lower with every step. When he reached his door, he swung his head around, nudging Melanie's boot.

"I'm still here," she said, kicking her feet loose from the stirrups.

When Melanie slid off, her legs felt like rubber. Collapsing against Jinx's sweat-drenched side, she sagged weakly to the ground.

Suddenly she felt strong arms lift her. It was Jazz. Ashleigh walked up behind Melanie and collected Jinx's reins.

"I'll walk him out for you, Mel," she said, looking at the colt. "I don't know what you did out there, but something's definitely changed with this horse."

Leaning against Jazz, Melanie closed her eyes as Jinx and Ashleigh set off down the barn aisle. She was still shaking as she considered the transformation she had just felt in the chestnut. Only minutes earlier Jinx had been a raging, conflicted colt. Now in his place was a different sort of horse altogether—a horse who maybe, just maybe, had discovered that he didn't need to fight the world. A horse who sensed that his true purpose was to run as he had been bred to do: all out and full speed ahead.

"Something just happened here," Melanie whispered to Jazz. "I got through to Jinx."

"All I know is that horse sure can run," Jazz replied, pulling her close to him.

Melanie nodded. "I told you he could. But he has to do it his way, that's all. Like Image. Well, kind of."

"Kind of like somebody else I know," Jazz murmured. "Now where are you off to?" he asked when Melanie pulled away.

"I'm going to tell Aunt Ashleigh that I'm keeping him," she said, determination welling up inside her.

Picking up her pace, Melanie hurried after Jinx. What lay ahead for her and the big red colt, she had no idea. She only knew that he was as great as she believed—and that it was up to her to bring it out for the racing world to see!

AP Photo

Seabiscuit and jockey George Woolf lead War Admiral and jockey
Charles Kurtsinger in the first turn at the race at Pimlico in Baltimore,
Md., on Nov. 1, 1938. Seabiscuit won and set a new track record.

SEABISCUIT

May 23, 1933–May 17, 1947

Seabiscuit was one of America's most unlikely racing
legends. The bay Thoroughbred was small as a colt,
unexceptional in appearance, erratic in behavior, and
unimpressive when he first began racing. But after a late
start, he began showing the promise of his illustrious
grandsire, the great Man o' War, when he won a number
of notable handicap races, including the Governor's
Handicap, the Bay Bridge Handicap, and the World's
Fair Handicap, breaking several track records along the
way. Seabiscuit raced all over the country, winning prestigious races that included the San Juan Capistrano
Handicap, the Marchbank Handicap, the Bay Meadows
Handicap, and the Hollywood Gold Cup. Despite recur-
ring knee problems and carrying what some felt were
unfair weights, the bay who was once nicknamed "the
Runt" earned national attention and the title of Horse of
the Year in 1938 when he won the Pimlico Special, beat-
ing Triple Crown-winner War Admiral in the spectacular
"Match of the Century." Seabiscuit was retired but then
came out of retirement to run in the Santa Anita Handicap, setting a new track record and becoming the all-time
leading money winner.

Karle Dickerson grew up riding, reading, writing, and dreaming about horses. This is the seventh horse book she has written. She has shown in hunters and dressage, worked at a Thoroughbred breeding farm, and has been on cattle drives in Wyoming. She and her family used to own a horse ranch, and have always had numerous horses and ponies. The latest include two Thoroughbreds off the track named Cezanne and Earl Gray, and a gray Welsh pony named Magpie.

WIN A YEAR'S SUBSCRIPTION TO
YOUNG RIDER MAGAZINE!

ENTER THE
Thoroughbred YOUNG RIDER MAGAZINE
SWEEPSTAKES!

COMPLETE THIS ENTRY FORM • NO PURCHASE NECESSARY

NAME: _____

ADDRESS: _____

CITY: _____ STATE: _____ ZIP: _____

PHONE: _____ AGE: _____

MAIL TO: THOROUGHBRED YOUNG RIDER MAGAZINE SWEEPSTAKES!
c/o HarperCollins, Attn.: Department AW
10 E. 53rd Street   New York, NY 10022

HarperEntertainment

17th Street Productions,
an Alloy Online, Inc., company

THOROUGHBRED 62 SWEEPSTAKES RULES
OFFICIAL RULES

1. No purchase necessary.

2. To enter, complete the official entry form or hand print your name, address, and phone number along with the words "Thoroughbred Free Magazine Sweepstakes" on a 3" x 5" card and mail to: HarperCollins, Attn.: Department AW, 10 E. 53rd Street, New York, NY 10022. Entries must be received by May 15, 2004. Enter as often as you wish, but each entry must be mailed separately. One entry per envelope. Partially completed, illegible, or mechanically reproduced entries will not be accepted. Sponsors are not responsible for lost, late, mutilated, illegible, stolen, postage-due, incomplete, or misdirected entries. All entries become the property of HarperCollins and will not be returned.

3. Sweepstakes open to all legal residents of the United States (excluding residents of Colorado and Rhode Island) who are between the ages of eight and sixteen by May 15, 2004, excluding employees and immediate family members of HarperCollins, Alloy Online, Inc., or 17th Street Productions, an Alloy Online, Inc. company, and their respective subsidiaries, and affiliates, officers, directors, shareholders, employees, agents, attorneys, and other representatives (individually and collectively), and their respective parent companies, affiliates, subsidiaries, advertising, promotion and fulfillments agencies, and the persons with whom each of the above are domiciled. Offer void where prohibited or restricted.

4. Odds of winning depend on total number of entries received. Approximately 100,000 entry forms have been distributed. All prizes will be awarded. Winners will be randomly drawn on or about May 30, 2004, by representatives of HarperCollins, whose decisions are final. Potential winners will be notified by mail, and a parent or guardian of the potential winners will be required to sign and return an affidavit of eligibility and release of liability within 14 days of notification. Failure to return the affidavit within the time period will disqualify the winner and another winner will be chosen. By acceptance of the prize, the winner consents to the use of his or her name, photographs, likeness, and personal information by HarperCollins, Alloy Online, Inc., and 17th Street Productions, an Alloy Online, Inc. company, for publicity and advertising purposes without further compensation except where prohibited.

5. Ten (10) Grand Prize Winners will receive a year's subscription to *Young Rider* magazine. HarperCollins reserves the right at its sole discretion to substitute another prize of equal or of greater value in the event this prize is unavailable. Approximate retail value totals $130.00.

6. Only one prize will be awarded per individual, family, or household. Prizes are nontransferable and cannot be sold or redeemed for cash. No cash substitute is available except at the sole discretion of HarperCollins for reasons of prize unavailability. Any federal, state, or local taxes are the responsibility of the winner.

7. Additional terms: By participating, entrants agree a) to the official rules and decisions of the judges, which will be final in all respects; and b) to release, discharge, and hold harmless HarperCollins, Alloy Online, Inc., and 17th Street Productions, an Alloy Online, Inc. company, and their affiliates, subsidiaries, and advertising promotion agencies from and against any and all liability or damages associated with acceptance, use, or misuse of any prize received in this sweepstakes.

8. To obtain the name of the winners, please send your request and a self-addressed stamped envelope (Vermont residents may omit return postage) to "Thoroughbred Free Magazine Winners List," c/o HarperCollins, Attn.: Department AW, 10 E. 53rd Street, New York, NY 10022.

SPONSOR: HarperCollins Publishers Inc.